FM

FM
Frequency For Murder

Dan Collins

In loving memory
Billie Collins
October 9, 1950 - February 14, 2020

Chapter 1

Midnight, a time when darkness rules the land. The overwhelming majority are fast asleep in their beds. Others enjoy the nightlife as they party till the sun comes up. Some work the late shift to help pay the next day's bills. Around the shade of darkness, KPDC radio continues to broadcast to the city throughout the night. Evening disc jockey Maniac Mike Martinez is getting ready to sign off.

"All right, my fellow creatures of the night, it's time for me to hit the floor, grab the door, and go home. Don't worry, my little night owls; I have somebody here to keep you company."

Maniac Mike spots a young woman entering the studio.

"Oh my goodness, I hope there's a camera in the studio because I just saw a gorgeous woman walk in. Anyway, stay tuned for Dr. Alex Birney and his new show, 'Midnight Confessions.' If he finds the studio before the show's over."

The young woman, slightly irritated, attempts to explain where the missing radio host is. Maniac Mike told her to speak in front of the microphone.

"I said, 'Dr. Alex Birney is right here, Maniac.' I'm looking forward to hosting the show."

Maniac's face turns a darker shade of red. He can't believe he set himself for this embarrassment.

"Folks, I am so sorry. I thought the host would be a gentleman. Instead, I found out that this lovely young lady is, in fact, Dr. Alex Birney, and she's hosting 'Midnight Confessions.'"

Maniac plays music while he gets ready to leave. Alex tries to smooth things over with him.

"It's not your fault, Maniac. I didn't believe the station manager told you 'Dr. Birney' is a woman."

Maniac is still hard on himself. "They should tell me who I'll work with before he or she comes in."

Dr. Birney gives Maniac a wry smile and the two shake hands. Maniac attempts to start over with his new colleague.

"What is Alex short for?"

Dr. Birney answers, "It's short for Alexandria."

"Let me guess, you're from Virginia, right?"

"No, a little further north. Michigan."

Maniac guesses why she came from Michigan.

"You're tired of the cold weather, aren't you?"

"It's the reason why I moved here."

"Perhaps, I'll save the small talk for next time. After the song is over, you'll go on the air."

Alex goes to her chair and puts on her headphones. As the song winds down, the sound engineer turns on her mike, and Alex Birney is ready to go.

"It's midnight, and it's time for you to confess. Welcome to 'Midnight Confessions,' I am your host, Dr. Alex Birney. If you have a question, please don't be afraid to call. Our phone lines are open until 6:00 AM; the number is 555-KPDC."

All of a sudden, the phone lines light up like a Christmas tree. Alex is happy to see it happen. She tackles topics with clients. This radio show would give Alex a chance to help caller's face issues they were afraid to talk about. Alex picks a button.

"Line 4, this is Dr. Birney, and you're on 'Midnight Confessions.' Who am I speaking to?"

The caller acts nervous.

"Is this K-K-K-KPDC radio?"

"It sure is, what is your name?"

"My n-n-name is Craig."

"Nice talking to you, Craig. What seems to be your problem?"

Craig explains despite his jitters.

"I'm a b-b-bit nervous with what I'm going to say."

"There's nothing to be nervous about, Craig. I'll be happy to help with your problem."

"Okay, my p-p-problem is with finding a woman."

Dr. Birney has addressed this issue dozens of times. She always has the simplest answer for those who struggle like Craig.

"Let me ask you a question, Craig. Do you go to bars?"

Craig is swift to reply. "N-n-no, I don't d-d-drink."

"Well, you can be a wingman to your friends whenever they go to a bar."

"I can't. Most of my friends left since high school."

Alex decides on another route. "Well, what about a health club or the supermarket?"

"I can't find the right time to work out and I can't shop during the day."

The kind doctor has one last suggestion. "What about where you work? You might find some great people with whom you have lots in common."

Craig gives this simple reply. "I d-d-don't believe my job will go well with the ladies."

"Where do you work?"

"I w-w-work in the morgue at County General."

Dr. Birney can't believe what Craig said. She offers him a piece of simple advice.

"Craig, here are my suggestions. The first is to try meeting more people when you're not at work."

Craig asks the doctor one more question. "W-w-what would be your other s-s-suggestion?"

"I recommend switching to decaf to get rid of the jitters."

"I'll t-t-try. Thank you, d-d-doctor."

"You're welcome, bye-bye."

Alex chooses her next caller.

"Line 1, you're on 'Midnight Confessions' with Dr. Alex Birney. Who am I talking to?"

The caller introduces herself.

"This is Ellen; I'm a long-time listener, first-time caller."

Dr. Birney becomes confused. "How can you be a long-time listener when this is my first show?"

"I'm a long-time listener to the station."

Dr. Birney sighs. "Oh, now I understand. What do you want to talk about, Ellen?"

"I'm seeing this guy at work, and he's so good-looking. I want to spend the rest of my days with him."

"Well, have you talked about this to him?"

"No, I'm too shy to know what to say to him."

Alex understands what Ellen is going through.

"My advice to you is don't rush things. Rushing to fall in love is like learning how to swim in the deep end."

Ellen gets the message clearly. "I understand what you mean, doctor. Thank you."

"You're welcome. Keep listening to 'Midnight Confessions,' Ellen."

Dr. Birney plays some music. She can't believe the responses from the callers: Kenny, the programming engineer, worries about Dr. Birney.

"Not bad for your first time, doc."

Dr. Birney gets concerned about her job. "Is it always like that all the time?"

"Not exactly, I've heard drunks calling the station trying to order pizzas."

"What do you say to them?"

"Sorry, we don't deliver."

The two laugh as the song ends. Dr. Birney goes back on the air.

"We're back with more of 'Midnight Confessions' here on KPDC. I'm Dr. Alex Birney, and the phone lines are open. Call 555-KPDC."

Dr. Birney chooses another caller.

"Line 5, you're on the air with Dr. Alex Birney, on 'Midnight Confessions.' Who is this calling?"

The caller hangs up. Alex thinks maybe she intimidated the caller.

"Either our last caller got too shy, or he called the show by mistake. Maybe our next caller won't be as shy as the previous one."

Alex goes to line 3.

"Line 3, you're on 'Midnight Confessions' with Dr. Alex Birney. Who am I talking to?"

The caller pauses.

"Is this Dr. Birney?"

"Yes it is, who am I talking to?"

"I don't want to say my name on the air. I wish to remain anonymous."

"I'm sorry, but if you wish to speak with me, I like to know who I am talking to."

The doctor's response does not put the stranger in a good mood.

"I don't like to give my name on the air."

"I'm sorry, rules are rules. I'll have to go to another caller."

Dr. Birney hangs the caller up and gives a message to her listeners.

"If anybody wants to make a call to the station, at least have a name."

Kenny monitors the phone calls so there wouldn't be any more 'anonymous' callers. Dr. Birney takes another call.

"When I take the next call, please tell me your name and what problem you have, so I can respond."

She hits line 2.

"Hello, line 2, this is Dr. Alex Birney, and you're on 'Midnight Confessions.' Who is this?"

The caller hesitates. "My name is... Bob."

"Hi, Bob. Is there something I can help you with?"

"Yes, there is."

"What seems to be the problem?"

Instantly, her caller's voice changes. "I want to know why you hung up on me!"

Alex panics. "Now you listen to me. I don't know how you got back through, but I will hang up again."

The caller delivered a threatening comeback.

"You hang up on me again; I will call back on every phone line."

"Goodbye, forever!"

Dr. Birney hangs up the phone and takes another call. The mysterious caller is on every line, leaving a diabolical laugh.

"I told you, Dr. Birney. You can't get rid of me."

"How are you doing this? What do you want from me!"

"It's a personal matter, doctor. Something I wanted to do to you a long time ago."

Alex's panic turns into fear. "I don't know what you're talking about."

"I do, Dr. Birney. When you find out, it'll be too late."

The caller hangs up. All the phone lines reverted to normal, and Kenny suggested postponing the call-ins. Alex insisted on making one more phone call to the police.

***

Moments later, the police arrived at the radio station, getting information from Alex and Kenny about what transpired. Detective Boyce Hammond, questions the young doctor.

"So let me get this straight. This caller called, and he threatened you on the air."

"Yes, I told that to the officers earlier. I want to know who sabotaged my first night?"

Hammond acts confident, "That's what we're trying to figure out, Ms. Birney."

"I prefer you to call me, 'Dr.' Birney, officer."

"Well, I'm a detective, Doctor." They look at each other.

Officer Gomez takes a look at the control room to see if anything's out of the ordinary. Hammond asks if there's any craziness that took place.

"There's nothing I could find that caused the phone lines to go berserk."

Storming towards the studio is Maxine Hathaway, station manager of KPDC Radio, who discovers that her station looks like it's run by Attila the Hun.

"I want to know why my presence was requested in the middle of the night just to see that my station looks like a crime scene."

Hammond tries to calm the manager down.

"Well, your station is now a crime scene now. We have it under control, Ms..."

"A crime scene. A crime scene! It's more like everybody wandering around when they should be doing their jobs."

Dr. Birney explains what happened to her.

"A guy called the station..."

Maxine interrupts her new employee. "Of course they call the station, they're supposed to do that."

Hammond goes on the offensive. "Not if the caller harassed your disc jockey."

Alex interjects, "Excuse me, but I am not a disc jockey. I'm the host of a radio call-in show."

Hammond turns to her. "Do you play music on your show, Doctor?"

"Yes, I do."

"Then you're a disc jockey."

Alex glares at the young detective. "Now you listen here; my job is to help callers with their problems over the air. I also do this in my private life."

"Why are you hosting a radio show?"

The station manager jumps in, "I'm one of her clients. Our old show had trouble getting a basic audience, and I believe she can get in touch with every night owl and graveyard shifter in the city."

Hammond turns his eyes back to the young psychologist.

"Has anybody threatened you like tonight, Doctor?"

"No, not like today."

Hammond feels that the case is going nowhere. He gives Alex his card and asks her to call him.

"If you deal with another spectacle like this, doctor. Please give me a call."

"I'd prefer if you call me Alex."

"Alright, Alex. I'd like to listen to your show to see how it's run."

Maxine doesn't like the idea. "I don't want the police involved in my station."

Alex disagrees with her boss. "What if the caller returns tonight?"

"I believe it's one of Maniac's practical jokes," Maxine responds.

"I don't think it's his style."

"I'll talk to him tonight. Until then postpone the calls, and just play some music 'til 6."

Alex is hurt. Her first day on the air was a mess and she's terrified and it's only a matter of time before the caller terrorizes her again.

Chapter 2

The next day, Boyce Hammond heads to the police station. He considers the information he got from Alex. At first; he thinks of it as a crazy, harmless prank. Alex doesn't seem to think so. The growing obsession with Alex's mystery caller keeps Hammond from a goodnight's sleep. Hammond's supervisor, Captain Thaddeus Railsback, gives his young detective a piece of advice.

"Why don't you go home and get some rest, son. You've been in this case all night."

"Sorry, Captain. My mind is on my witness."

"Dr. Alex Barney, right?"

"Birney, sir. Dr. Alex Birney."

"She's the woman who just took over the midnight show?"

"Yes sir, 'Midnight Confessions.' People call in and tell her about their problems."

"I can tell it's a lot cheaper than going to an actual shrink."

Hammond couldn't argue with that. "It sure beats driving to one, too."

Railsback tries to figure out what happened. "You're saying she has a caller stalking her?"

"He did more than stalk her, sir. He somehow showed up on all five phone lines at the same time."

Railsback is confused. "How can someone be on all five phone lines at the same time?"

"I'm trying to figure out how he did it, Captain."

The phone rings on Hammond's desk. Hammond picks it up right away.

"Hammond speaking."

Maxine Hathaway is on the other line. She thinks she knows how to capture Alex's obsessed caller. Hammond listens to what Maxine says, and he thinks Alex needs to hear this as well.

"Where could I find Dr. Birney?"

Maxine has the number for Dr. Birney's office; she gives the young detective the number over the phone. After the conversation, Hammond calls Dr. Birney. He gets the voicemail.

"Hello, you've reached the office of Dr. Alex Birney. I am away for the time; please leave your name and message and I'll call you as soon as I can. Thank you."

At the tone, Hammond leaves a message for Alex.

"Dr. Birney, this is Detective Hammond. I'm calling you about the incident at the radio station. I gave you my business card, so please call the number. Bye."

Hammond hangs up the phone after completing the message. He worries about what Alex's stalker is planning and when he plans to strike next.

***

Moments later, Detective Hammond heads off to KPDC Radio for an appointment with Maxine Hathaway. He stopped at the receptionist's desk and finds her reading a trashy romance novel that has probably been on the desk for 20 years. Hammond cleared his throat, getting her attention.

"Excuse me, Miss. I'm here to see Ms. Hathaway."

The receptionist keeps reading her novel and does not recognize the young detective.

"Who are you supposed to be?"

She blows a bubble as Hammond reveals his detective badge. The bubble pops in the receptionist's face. Alex arrives at the station, and she isn't happy to see Hammond at the reception desk.

"I got your message, Detective. I am not in the mood to answer any of your questions."

Hammond presses on, "I'm here to talk to your boss. If it concerns the station, it also concerns you."

Alex doesn't like what Hammond said; she would like to see her mysterious caller in jail due to the cruel practical joke. Maxine arrives to bring them to her office.

"Alex, are you and the detective getting to know each other?"

The doctor responds, "This isn't a dating service, Ms. Hathaway. What is Mr. Hammond doing here?"

"I invited him. I want to know who made those threats over the air, and so should you."

Maxine tells the psychologist and the detective to come to her office. As they all sit down, Maxine outlines her plan for stopping Alex's stalker.

"Now, Alex, the reason why I wanted to bring Detective. I'm sorry, I forgot your name."

"It's Hammond, ma'am. Detective Boyce Hammond."

"Of course." Maxine turns to Alex. "As I was saying, I invited Detective Hammond to my office because I want him to see how the station is run."

"Is he co-hosting my show now?"

Hammond gave Alex a simple answer. "No, but I'll help your engineer monitor your calls for tonight's broadcast."

"What do you mean, 'monitor the phone calls'?"

"You said the person who called you last night threatened you over the air."

"Yes, I did."

"Your boss thinks we should find out where the calls are coming from. When we figure that out, we'll bust him."

Alex likes the idea, but she has one problem regarding the phone sting.

"What if the caller calls some other way, like from a phone booth?"

Hammond has a simple answer. "Impossible. There hasn't been a phone booth in San Dimas in the last ten years."

"Okay, I don't like where this is going, but I'll listen to the two of you."

Maxine has another concern. "I think Maniac is the one who played the prank on Alex."

Hammond says. "I will talk to Maniac before 'Midnight Confessions' starts. I believe it's not his M.O."

"M.O.?"

Alex explains to her boss. "Modus Operandi, I took criminal justice in college,"

Hammond asks, "Where did you go to school?"

"Michigan State. I came out west after I graduated."

Hammond's surprised. "How long have you been here?"

"Six years."

"It beats dealing with the cold, doesn't it?"

Alex sighs. She gets the question whenever she meets someone new.

"This city has its perks."

Maxine interrupts this potential love connection. "If I'm not mistaken, this is a radio station, not a dating service. The idea is to find out where the calls are coming from. All we have to do is trace the line to where he's calling and nail the sucker!"

Hammond threw his two cents in: "Our boys can trace the call once we hear your stalker's voice."

Alex worried, "What do I do if he calls?"

Hammond gave his best idea to his witness. "Talk to him."

"Talk to him?"

"Get the creep to stall long enough for us to trace the phone call."

Maxine throws in her two cents. "Once we get the phone number, we'll find out where he's calling from, and arrest the S.O.B."

Alex doesn't share Hammond and Maxine's enthusiasm. However, she wants this nightmare to end as soon as possible.

After the meeting, Hammond catches up with Dr. Birney. He knows the young psychologist is not happy with his plan.

"Dr. Birney, could I ask you a question?"

"Make it quick; I have to go home and get to bed."

"But it's 2:30 in the afternoon."

"I know, but since I started doing the radio show, I have to find a balance with my regular job. So, I have to go to bed in the afternoon."

Hammond understands, but he still needs to ask Alex a question.

"How come you don't like our plan for capturing your obsessed caller?"

Alex had the only explanation. "It's hard to find one phone number in a population with over a million people."

"Yes, but we have the tools and the talent to zero in on who's calling you."

Alex isn't sure how the trap will be set, and when the rat will take the bait. Hammond would have to earn her trust.

"Look, Dr. Birney, please do your job tonight so that I can do mine."

"I'll try, but I don't want to end up as live bait."

"Go home and sleep on it, okay?"

As Hammond leaves the radio station, Alex starts worrying. She knows her on-air stalker is out there somewhere. The idea of even one call from him terrifies her. Alex heads for her car and drives down to her apartment.

***

Around midnight, Alex returns to KPDC radio. As she enters the hall, she looks at the lights on the ceiling flicker on and off.

"Hello?"

Her voice echoed throughout the building. Nobody answered.

"Anybody here?"

Nothing but silence. Alex shudders and heads to the studio, and as she sits on the chair, she sees the phone with all five buttons lit up. Alex takes a deep breath, picks up the headset and answers the first call.

"Hello, you're on Midnight Confessions with Dr. Alex Birney. Who am I talking to?"

She hears a familiar voice she doesn't want to hear.

"Remember me, Dr. Birney?"

Alex reflexively hangs up the phone, and answers the next line.

"Hello..."

The caller interrupts her.

"It's not nice to hang up on me, Alex."

Dr. Birney becomes angry.

"Now, you listen here, you worthless piece of ---."

"Ah, ah, ah! Watch the language, doc. A pretty girl like you shouldn't say any foul words."

Alex furiously slams the phone down and yanks out the cord. She heads down to the engineer's room and finds Kenny laying on the ground, dead. The phone in the studio continues to ring. Alex rushes out of the station to see a shadow of a man with a knife in his hand ready to strike. Alex screams louder than any alarm. She's still screaming as she wakes up in her bed, crying. It's 10 PM, and Dr. Alexandria Birney needs to get ready for work, and the opportunity to catch her obsessed caller.

Chapter 3

It is now 10:30 PM, and Dr. Alex Birney heads off to KPDC radio for another session of 'Midnight Confessions'. Her first day on the job ended in disaster because of an obsessed caller who apparently knows her well. She wonders why the stranger would call her and why he wants to be with her. Was there somebody from her past that she'd forgotten about, perhaps intentionally? Alex puts her problem behind her as she arrives at the station. Detective Hammond parks beside her. Alex flinches, thinking that Hammond is the stalker.

"You shouldn't scare me like that. I'm buying a can of mace after work."

Hammond is no stranger to apologies. "I'm sorry I frightened you, Doctor. I hope you're ready for this."

"Nothing will make me happier than seeing that caller behind bars."

"You shouldn't worry about it. Our tech boys arrived 10 minutes ago."

"Did you talk to Maniac?"

"I talked with Maniac earlier today."

"What did he say about what happened?"

Hammond knew Maniac had an alibi. "It turns out he was stuck in traffic on his way home."

"I know Maniac is innocent," Alex replied, "he doesn't own a cell phone."

Hammond acts shocked.

"What do you mean he doesn't own a cell phone?"

"He called my office earlier today. It's from a landline; he gave me his explanation."

Hammond now has one less suspect to worry about. "At least we both know he didn't do it. Maxine would not be happy about it if he had."

"Detective, Maxine won't be happy if Maniac hasn't done it, either."

The two laugh as they enter the building and head to the elevator en route to the studio. Maniac is working the mike as the tech team works in the engineer's room, setting the trap for Alex's obsessed caller.

"Okay, night owls. I see Dr. Birney is in our studio, so it's time for me to hit the floor, grab the door, and go home."

Hammond chuckles to himself, watching Maniac getting ready to call it a night. Maniac finishes the broadcast.

"Stay tuned for 'Midnight Confessions' coming up next. I hope and pray this edition is less interesting than the last."

Alex rolls her eyes at Maniac, but she knows this is the first step of putting last night's nightmare to rest.

"Until then, this is your friendly neighborhood Maniac reminding you the asylum is now closed. This is KPDC, the voice of San Dimas."

Maniac plays some music as he takes his headset off. He speaks with Alex and Hammond.

"I'm sorry about what I said, Alex. I did that out of character."

"It's okay, the sooner this ends, the better."

"I'll be happy to find the creep myself and beat him up for you."

Hammond chuckles, "I know you would do that for Alex, but the law won't allow it."

Maniac doesn't like Hammond's comment, but he understands. Officer Feldman from the tech lab tells Hammond that the program for finding Alex's stalker is up and running. He tells Alex that once her mystery caller calls in, they'll trace the phone signal, find and arrest the psycho caller. Hammond gives Alex one more piece of advice.

"Remember, when your caller calls you, keep stalling 'til we find out where he's calling from."

"I get it. It's time to put this nightmare to end once and for all."

With midnight fast approaching, Dr. Birney heads to her chair, puts her headset on, and gets ready to go on air.

"It's midnight, and it's time for you to confess. Welcome to 'Midnight Confessions.' I'm your host, Dr. Alex Birney. Do you have any secrets? I'll be happy to take your calls. The phone lines are open until 6 AM, and the number is 555-KPDC."

Over in the engineer's room, Kenny puts some callers on hold while Hammond waits for the mysterious caller to pop up. The phone lines are jam-packed, it's time for the Doctor to take action.

"I see the callers are ready. I am going to take the first call."

Alex hits the first blinking button.

"Line one, you're on 'Midnight Confessions' with Dr. Alex Birney. Who am I speaking to?"

"Hello, Doctor, this is Paul. I'm a little nervous about calling here."

"Paul, there is nothing wrong with being nervous. What do you want to talk about?"

"In April, my wife was killed by a drunk driver. I haven't been able to pick up the pieces back since."

"I am sorry for your loss, Paul. Have you tried to go back into the dating pool?"

"No, I haven't got the time to meet somebody. I also have a five-year-old son who keeps me on my toes. He misses his mom and I'm not sure how to approach this."

"What you're saying is you don't know how to find somebody who would not only love you but also your son."

"Yes, of course. I feel like I'm pressured by everybody to go back into dating."

Dr. Birney gave Paul her advice. "I know that dating is difficult for someone who's dealing with loss. And people don't like to hurry at finding another chance at love."

Over at the engineer's room, Hammond listened as Alex gives her caller advice. He believes his own job has kept him from having a relationship. From his eyes, he saw something different in Dr. Birney and hopes he can find the caller, to show his appreciation.

Alex continues her advice to Paul. "When you go back to dating, don't try to rush things. Take your time to get to know somebody before going to the next step."

"Thank you, Dr. Birney. I'll keep your advice in mind."

"Call me back with an update."

"Will do, good night, Doctor."

"Good night."

Hammond verifies that the first caller wasn't Alex's stalker. He thinks maybe the stalker is waiting for her first blunder. Alex picks her next caller.

"Line 4, you're on 'Midnight Confessions' with me, Dr. Alex Birney. Who do I have the pleasure of speaking to?"

"Hello, Dr. Birney, my name is Nicole."

"Hi, Nicole, what seems to be the problem?"

"Well, I'm having an on-again, off-again relationship with my boyfriend."

"Are you currently with him?"

Nicole has no hesitation in answering Alex's question. "No. Last week, a friend of mine saw him kissing another girl."

"Have you talked to him?"

"I have, but it's happened before and he always says it wasn't him. I even went as far as placing a tracker on his cell phone."

"Did you catch him cheating, Nicole?"

"You'd better believe it. I followed him and saw him kissing another girl in her apartment. Doctor, I don't want to end up on one of those talk shows with a polygraph. I do love him, but I don't know what to do."

Alex gives Nicole a simple answer.

"I believe you know the answer yourself. If he's cheating on you, then I believe you deserve somebody better. Plan a girl's trip with you and your friends. You'll find somebody who'll love you for you."

Nicole suggests, "My friend has a bachelorette party in Acapulco."

Alex likes Nicole's idea. "That would be a good start."

"Thank you, Doctor. I'll call the hotel first thing in the morning."

"You do that, remember to take time for yourself as well."

"Will do, gracias."

Alex tells her audience she'll play some music as she takes a break. Hammond thinks this evening is going nowhere. He wonders if the caller will call and harass Alex. Or maybe, as he originally thought, the calls are nothing more than he thought in the first place: a harmless practical joke. However, Hammond begins to worry.

"Kenny, around what time did the mysterious caller call last night?"

Kenny gives the young detective a rough estimate. "I say about a half-hour into the program."

"I'm thinking the next call she'll pick up will be our guy."

"We now have five different lines calling from the same phone. The only way we'll find the creep is when she pushes the button."

The song is over, and Alex is back on the air, ready to take another call.

"Welcome back, I'm Dr. Alex Birney, and you're listening to 'Midnight Confessions' on KPDC radio. The call-in number is 555-KPDC. Lets go to line two, who's been waiting patiently."

Alex pushes the line 2 button.

"Line 2, this is Dr. Alex Birney on 'Midnight Confessions.' Who is this?"

"Hello, Dr. Birney. Remember me?"

The caller is back. Hammond and Kenny trace the phone call. Alex does her best to stall her obsessed caller.

"Of course, I remember you. Bob, isn't it?"

"No, but that's how I got your attention yesterday."

As Alex continues talking to her obsessed caller, Hammond looks for the number from where he's calling from. Hammond wants Alex to talk a little longer.

Alex asks her caller the hard question. "Why do you keep calling me?"

The caller is in charge. "Uh-uh! I make the rules around here, toots. Not you."

"Who do you think you are?"

"I'm a voice from your past, Alex. I will find you, and when I do, I'm going to pick up where I left off."

"You don't know a thing about me."

"I know everything about you, and I can't wait to find you again."

"Again? How are you going to find me, you creep!"

The caller figures out why Alex is asking so many questions.

"No! This is not the way I want it."

The caller quickly hangs up on Alex. Hammond is not happy at all; he wanted Alex to talk to her caller a little longer. Suddenly, a number appears on the screen. A smile runs across Hammond's face.

"I got you. I got you!"

Hammond contacts the tech lab to check on the phone number that he got from the scrambler. He tells himself he has to put the caller somewhere he'll never find or hurt Alex again. Alex sees Hammond coming out of Kenny's engineering room.

"Did you get the number?"

"I sure did, we're getting the info from the phone number right away. He's not going to bother you again."

As Hammond leaves the studio, he gets a call from the tech saying who has the number and the location. He gets in his car and heads to his destination.

**

Moments later, Hammond arrives at an apartment complex two miles south of the station. Two police cars arrive as backup. Officer Ridgely gazes at the scene.

"It's quiet."

"Too quiet," said Officer Elliot, Ridgely's partner, as he turns to Hammond. "Are you sure this is the right address?"

"I'm sure this is the right location," Hammond says with confidence. "The guys from tech tied the phone number to here. After tonight, he won't be calling Alex again. Now follow me."

The trio of police officers enter the apartment complex. A guard asks them why they're here in the middle of the night. Hammond explains the situation. The guard points to the suspected apartment. As they arrive, Hammond knocks at the door. A groggy young man in his pajamas opens the door. Detective Hammond asks the tenant a few questions.

"Are you Nicholas Bosley?"

Nicholas wipes the sleep out of his eyes. "Yes, I'm Nicholas Bosley."

Hammond shows Nicholas the phone number. "Is this your phone number?"

"Yes, it is, officer."

Hammond has one thing to say to the sleepy head. "Get dressed, you're going downtown."

"Hey, man. What's the charge?"

"You're under arrest for stalking over the phone."

"I got to be at work at 5:30 in the morning."

"It can wait. Get dressed and come with us."

Nicholas goes back to his room and gets dressed. As they're leaving, Bosley warns the police.

"You are making a serious mistake, Detective."

"Tell that to Dr. Birney."

"Who?"

"Let's go."

Officer Ridgley read Nicholas his Miranda rights as the police leave the apartment. Hammond believes that with the stalker caught, Alex's nightmare would be over. He's unaware that it's only the beginning.

Chapter 4

As the night becomes the day, Detective Hammond interrogates Nicholas Bosley about stalking Dr. Alex Birney over-the-air on 'Midnight Confessions.' Nicholas keeps repeating the same answer.

"I told you I was asleep for the past three hours before you arrested me. I've never called the radio station."

Hammond doesn't budge. "Why did we find your number on our tracer last night?"

"Are you spying on me?"

"We were tracking who called Dr. Murphy's show last night."

Officer Ridgely came in from tech and tells Hammond the news.

"We have to let him go, Boyce. He's clean."

Boyce can't believe what he heard. "What do you mean, he's clean?"

Ridgely explains, "We contacted his cell phone provider, and they provided his call log from the last thirty days."

"None of the calls he made involve the radio station?"

"Not one call, sir."

Nicholas feels exonerated, but he's not happy.

"Can I please leave the station? I'm late for work because of you turkeys."

Hammond asks, "Where do you work? We'll give you a ride there."

"I work with the road crew doing repairs on West Arrow."

Ridgely asks, "What do you do for your crew?"

"I hold the stop sign. I'm the guy who keeps cars moving and stopping in nearly 100-degree weather."

Hammond tells Ridgely to take Nicholas back to work and explain the situations to his supervisor. As Nicholas Bosley leaves the interrogation room with Officer Ridgely, Boyce Hammond sits down and pounds his fist on the table with a solid thud. Captain Railsback takes a concerned look at his top detective.

"I had that scoundrel, and he slipped through my fingers."

Railsback understands what Hammond is going through. "Boyce, don't let this case get to you."

"I'm afraid it has gotten to me."

As Hammond stares at the surface of the table, he remembers what the caller said on yesterday's show.

"This is not what he wanted. Ugh! I should have known!"

Railsback wonders, "What's the matter?"

Hammond explains to his supervisor, "The last words the caller said to Alex last night. He knew we were tracking him."

"I don't understand what you're saying."

"When Alex's stalker called in, we trace the number from where he called."

Railsback now understands what his detective is going. "Alex tried talking to him a little longer so you can find the phone number."

"Exactly, when he hung up, that's when I got Bosley's number. He knew. He must have a scrambler to make sure he uses someone else's number and not his own."

"So, maybe he's a technological genius at the station?"

"It's a possibility. I'll contact the station if anybody knows the technology. I don't think it was Kenny."

Railsback thinks of another thing. "The person who's harassing Alex made it sound like he has a history with her."

"You mean like an ex-boyfriend?"

"Maybe. Why do you think people like Alex move to San Dimas?"

"I believe they want to start over."

"They move west because they like the warm sunshine instead of the cold up north in places like Minnesota."

"Dr. Birney came from Michigan, Captain."

"Same thing."

"I'll head to Alex's apartment and tell her the bad news."

Hammond takes the call log and heads off to Alex's apartment. Railsback suspects that this case is becoming more serious than he thought.

***

At her apartment, Alex Birney is starting her morning off by doing yoga. Alex has been doing yoga since her college days. Her apartment is quiet, which helps her focus her mind along with her body. As Alex goes into a downward-facing dog, she hears a knock on the door.

Alex heads to the door, "Who is it?"

A familiar voice answers from outside.

"It's Detective Hammond, may I come in?"

Alex opens the door, "Come in."

Hammond enters Alex's apartment; he likes how she takes care of the place.

"This is nice. Do you spruce up for company?"

"Oh, no. I clean on the weekends," Alex replied. "Would you like a cup of coffee? I'm about to fix myself one."

"No, thank you. I had some this morning."

Hammond looks at a picture of Alex graduating from Michigan State University. He asks, "Did you live around Lansing all your life?"

"No, I lived a little further east. Tecumseh."

"I don't think I've heard of Tecumseh."

"It's named after an Indian Chief. I graduated with honors from Tecumseh High School, and then I went to Michigan State with a major in psychology."

Hammond looked at a picture of Alex with another person on the shelf. The other person's head has been torn off.

"Who's the guy in the picture?"

"What are you talking about?"

Hammond shows Alex the photo. Alex answers.

"Oh, that. He's nobody."

Alex knows why the young detective is here.

"I heard you captured my obsessed collar last night."

Hammond hates to disappoint Alex. "It's what I came here to talk to you about."

Alex swings from happiness to despair with Hammond's explanation.

"Are you saying that the guy you arrested is not my caller?"

Hammond had one simple answer. "No, he isn't, and we had to let him go."

"So, the man who keeps calling me is still on the loose?"

"Yes. I'm sorry, Alex."

Alex drops the coffee mug and it shatters on the floor. She knows her stalker is still roaming around the area, hoping to kill her. Overwhelmed, Alex falls into Hammond's arms with tears pouring down her face. Hammond has to be firm but shows compassion to his client.

"Alex, I swear, I'll find the guy who's stalking you," he says as he pats her back. "I'll make sure he'll never get his slimy hands on you."

Alex's telephone rings. Knowing she's upset. Hammond disentangles himself and answers the phone for her.

"Hello," he answers. "What do you mean, who is this! This is Detective Hammond."

It turns out to be Maxine Hathaway on the phone, and she is mad. She demands to talk to Alex; Hammond tells her that Alex can't come to the phone. Alex tells the detective she'll talk to her boss. Hammond offers Alex the phone.

"Hello," she answers. "Yes, I understand. I'll be there in twenty minutes."

Hammond gives Alex a funny look. He shows himself out. Once he's gone, Alex gets in the shower. She weeps, knowing her obsessed caller is out there, and he won't stop until he sees Alex Birney dead.

Chapter 5

Hammond heads back to the police station. He wants to tell Alex that the bad news upset him more than it did her. As he gets to his desk, an officer tells him Captain Railsback wanted to see him in his office on the double. Hammond knocks on the Captain's door.

"Come in," the Captain says.

Hammond opens the door with a concerned look on his face.

"You wanted to see me, sir?"

"I do, Boyce. Please have a seat."

As Hammond sits down, Railsback asks.

"How did she handle the news?"

"Terribly," Hammond sighs. "I thought we got the creep last night."

"I understand, Boyce," Railsback says. "What I don't know is how he got us to pick up the wrong guy?"

Hammond remembers what the caller said. It's not the way he wanted it. Knowing he's playing by the obsessed caller's own set of rules frustrates him.

"Whatever he does, Captain, he's always a step ahead."

"Like a real-life horror movie," Railsback replied. "Except this time, we're dealing with a high-tech boogeyman."

"Have the guys from the tech lab figured out how our caller did all of this?"

"So far, they don't know how it's done."

Hammond has one idea that might fit.

"Do you think our mystery caller knows how to tap a telephone on more than one line?"

Captain Railsback suggests one hypothesis, "Maybe he had experience at a tech school."

Hammond also has one more theory. "Or, maybe he learned it from the military."

"Of course, some soldiers learn how to hack into enemy phone lines when they're in combat."

"I'll ask Miss Hathaway if somebody with military experience has tried to apply for a radio job."

"Do that. In the meantime, I'll check for any news from the tech lab."

As Hammond gets ready to leave the Captain's office, a spark enters his mind.

"I almost forgot something."

"What is it, Boyce?"

"Can you contact the police stations in East Lansing and Tecumseh, Michigan?"

"Sure, what do you have in mind?"

"I believe something happened to Alex before she came here."

"It may take a couple of days to get info from Lansing. What other town did you say, Boyce?"

"Tecumseh, sir."

"I never heard of it. Sounds like an Indian name."

"It is, sir."

"I'll see what they can dig up."

"Thank you, sir," Hammond says as he leaves the Captain's office. With the stalker on the loose, he knows he must start from the beginning.

***

Hammond arrives at KPDC radio. He goes to the reception desk. The receptionist contacts Maxine, who tells her to let him in. As the detective gets to Maxine's office, he ffinds her talking to Alex. Maxine had one announcement.

"The show is on hiatus."

Alex is stunned. "What do you mean, 'on hiatus'?"

Maxine replies, "I can't have somebody threaten our on-air staff while he's out on the loose."

Hammond gently explains to his client, "Alex, your safety is more important than the show. You'll have to focus on your day job until the caller is caught."

Maxine replies, "Until then, the only person working in the studio will be Kenny. No others will be at the station after midnight."

Maxine's telephone rings. She doesn't like interrupted meetings. She turns on the speaker mode and gives the receptionist a piece of her mind.

"Look, Wendy. I thought I told you to hold all my calls."

The person on the other line hisses, "I'm not your receptionist, you old hag!"

Alex is in complete shock. Her obsessed caller is calling Maxine's private phone number. Maxine Hathaway goes ballistic.

"How dare you call me?"

The caller answers, "I know Alex is in your office. I also know Detective Hammond is there too."

"I'm here, creep. What do you want?" Hammond demands.

"Just a simple answer, detective," the caller replies. "How did it feel to be outsmarted by me? I tricked you into arresting the wrong man."

The caller lets out a laugh, making Hammond furious.

"You listen to me, you ungrateful punk. You think you won the fight?"

"I'm just getting started, detective," the caller says. "The way I see it, I only won round 1, and when I'm through embarrassing you, I'm going to knock you out; and take what is mine."

Alex argues. "You think those scare tactics frighten me?"

"No, my dear Alex, they're not 'tactics'. I expect you to face your fear head on."

"Who do you think you are!"

"Don't you remember the last time you saw me in East Lansing?"

"I don't know what you're talking about."

"Maybe you remember me when we went to Tecumseh High School. I can't wait to see you again when I come to kill you."

The caller laughs at Alex as he hangs up the phone. Hammond looked at the number on the caller ID, hoping this time the caller is as good as caught. When they look at the number, it's clear where the call came from.

"That's Maniac's line. I'm going to fire him."

Hammond tries to slow things down.

"I don't want you to jump to conclusions yet."

"What do you mean by jumping to conclusions?"

Alex says, "The last time we did that, we arrested the wrong man."

"I don't care what you two think," Maxine replies, "I'm tired of Maniac's practical jokes."

Hammond thinks the best way to handle the situation is to leave Maxine's office.

Maxine shouts, "Where do you think you're going!"

Hammond turns around and gives Maxine his only solution.

"I'm going to do my job, Ms. Hathaway. I'm going to talk with Maniac."

***

After leaving the radio station, Hammond goes to the home of Maniac Mike Martinez. He suspects the nighttime disc jockey is Alex's obsessed caller, but he wants to make sure Maxine's conclusions are not what he thinks they are. Hammond knows that Maniac's home, and he knocks on the door. Maniac heads to the door, loudly cursing up a storm. He opens the door to see Detective Hammond standing outside.

"Do you mind if I come in?"

"No, not at all," he replies. "Come on in."

Hammond enters Maniac's apartment and notices that he's not much into housekeeping.

"I'm sorry about the mess."

"That's not why I came here," Hammond replies. "I want to know if you called Maxine's office earlier today while she was with Alex."

Maniac knew what Hammond was implying.

"I'm sorry, detective, but I never call Maxine's office at all. No matter how much I hate her guts."

"What caused you and Maxine to be at odds with one another?"

Maniac explains, "You know how most shock jocks are, they always have some sick scheme to gain fans."

"Do you have an example?"

"Are you kidding? I have tons of examples, like this one time, we had a bikini contest on Memorial Day..."

"I believe I know what you mean," Hammond replies. "The girls got loud cheers, and the crowd had too many beers."

"You know it," Maniac says with a laugh. "I didn't think the contest would be featured on a late-night infomercial."

"Some of the girls flashed on camera?"

"You better believe it! It's like they called in a state militia after all the craziness."

"Maxine had to be furious after that fiasco."

"I saw the vein on her forehead got bigger by the minute."

Hammond tells Maniac about what happened in Maxine's call with Alex's caller, who appeared to be using Maniac's line. Maniac isn't happy, but he has a decent answer.

"I don't own a cell phone. I only have a landline phone."

"If we can contact your phone company and if there's nothing from the call logs," Hammond says, "we'll tell Maxine you're not Alex's obsessed caller."

"Detective, I told you before, and I'll tell you again for the last time," Maniac replies. "I am not Alex's obsessed caller. I don't even know her phone number."

All of a sudden, an idea popped into Maniac's mind.

"Arrest me."

"Are you crazy? I can't put you in jail for something you haven't done."

"I know, but Maxine thinks I'm guilty. If I'm in jail, and the calls continue..."

Hammond understands what Maniac is saying. Maxine thinks he's the culprit, and she wants to see Maniac locked up. Maniac has one chance to prove his innocence. Hammond places the handcuffs on the nighttime shock jock and reads him his rights. Maniac heads off to the station in Detective Hammond's car.

Maxine gets excited when she hears the news of Maniac's arrest. She calls to ask Alex to come to the studio tonight. Alex knows that Maniac would never harass her, but the culprit is still at large. With Maniac in jail, her stalker now knows Alex Birney will be easy prey.

Chapter 6

News on the arrest of Maniac Mike Martinez spread like wildfire all over San Dimas. Reporters hover over the San Dimas Police Department like moths attracted to bright lights. Captain Railsback isn't happy with all the publicity.

"Hammond, I spent the last two hours talking to reporters," he says to his top detective. "I don't know why you have said nothing to them."

"Oh, I will, Captain." Hammond says, "once I have all the facts."

Railsback becomes confused. "What do you mean, Boyce?"

"I contacted Maniac's phone company, got the call logs from them, and not one call was made to Maxine's office from that number."

"Are you saying that Maxine wants revenge for what he did on the air?"

"My only explanation is that shock jocks and conservative radio managers don't mix."

"You don't believe Maniac Mike is making the phone calls on Dr. Birney."

"The phone company said he didn't, Captain," Hammond says. "Did you get any reports from Tecumseh?"

"Not yet, Boyce," Railsback says in frustration. "You need to ask Alex more about what happens to her."

Officer Hatch tells Hammond that Maxine is calling on line 3. Hammond takes the call from his desk.

"Maxine, I know you're having your jollies now, but..."

Maxine interrupts the detective in a fit of rage.

"I don't know how Maniac is doing this behind bars, but I'm angry!"

"Well, this time, you don't have to blame Maniac, Ms. Hathaway," Hammond says. "We have your shock-jock in custody."

"Then how on Earth did that psycho caller call my office, AGAIN!"

"WHAT!"

Maxine explains the problem to Hammond. "Two hours after you arrested Maniac, I got a fax saying, 'I removed the cause, but not the symptom.'"

"It means Maniac is innocent," Hammond replies, "Unless you have something to hide, Ms. Hathaway?"

Maxine let out a slew of obscenities over the phone. Hammond's only defense is to hold the phone away from his ear. Maxine's loud rant continues.

"Are you holding the phone away from your ear? How dare you put the phone away from your ear while I'm talking to you!"

Hammond rebuts, "How dare you continue to accuse your disc jockey of a crime he never committed?"

"How dare you!"

"How dare you!"

Hammond takes a breath and tries to explain to Maxine what's going on.

"I believe that whosoever called the station in the last few days must have had experience with electronics."

"You mean like interrupting phone calls without the caller's knowledge?" Maxine says, "Oh, my God. What if he's eavesdropping on this conversation?"

"If he is, contact Captain Railsback here at the station, and I'll talk to you in person. We'll tell you what to look out for."

"Let Maniac go; I'm not pressing charges."

"I'll tell Maniac the good news, Miss Hathaway. Bye-bye."

After his talk with Maxine, Hammond goes to the cell to release Maniac.

"Good news, Maniac. You're free to go. Maxine won't press charges."

"What made her change her mind?"

"Our caller faxed a nasty note while you were in here."

"A fax?" Maniac says in confusion, "That's not the way he plays."

"What do you mean by that?"

"I mean, who uses a fax machine nowadays?"

"Some people still do it for work."

"Can you send a fax from your computer?"

Hammond never thought of this. "I believe it's possible. My guess is somebody must have gotten Maxine's fax number the same way they got the phone number from Alex's show."

"Boy, I'd like to spend some time alone with that creep." Maniac says, "He won't be able to call the station at all when I'm through with him."

Hammond has a better solution, "Look, I know you really want to put Alex's caller in traction, but it would lead to serious charges."

"What kind of 'serious charges'?"

"Anything   from   assault   and   battery   to manslaughter."

Maniac weighs his options, but decides he doesn't want to stay in jail one minute longer.

"When you find the creep, give him one for me."

"Will do," Hammond replies, "I'll give you a ride home."

"That's nice of you, Detective," Maniac says. "My ex-girlfriend wouldn't do that for me, especially if I landed in jail."

***

Hammond heads back to the radio station after taking Maniac home, where Maxine is waiting with the fax she got from Alex's obsessed caller.

"I thought this was one of Maniac's twisted jokes," she says, "but this came when Maniac was in your custody."

"I didn't think he would send you a fax," Hammond replies. "I thought he called you the same way he called Alex."

"Alex doesn't know about this, does she?"

"I don't think she does," Hammond answers, "I still think this may be one practical joke gone too far."

"Detective, it's already gone too far. I want to know who's responsible for this crap."

"I know, Ms. Hathaway. So does Alex."

Hammond leaves Maxine's office, concerned. He knows the only person who can point to the caller's identity. He picks up his cell phone and contacts Alex's office. Her secretary answers the phone.

"Dr. Birney's office."

"Yes, this is Detective Hammond with the San Dimas Police Department. I'd like to speak to Dr. Birney, please."

"I'm sorry, Dr. Birney is at lunch, she won't be back for another half-hour."

"Do you know where she's at?"

"Not really, where she goes to lunch varies from day-to-day."

Hammond needs to see Alex as soon as possible, but all he can do is to give her secretary a message.

"Tell Dr. Birney that Detective Hammond called, and she needs to call him as soon as possible."

"Do you have a number for her to call, Detective?"

Hammond gave the secretary his cell phone number.

"555-0219."

The secretary jots down Hammond's phone number and tells the young detective she'll give Alex the message.

"Please get her to call me."

"I'll do that."

"Thank you, bye-bye."

As Hammond heads to his car, his cell phone rings. Alex responds to Hammond's message.

"I got your message, Detective," she says. "Is there anything wrong?"

"No, I need to talk to you."

"I think I've given you enough information about my caller. I don't know what else you need from me."

"I want to know about Michigan and if there's somebody you're trying to get away from without putting my colleagues or me in a wild goose chase as we try to read your mind."

Alex lets her guard down.

"Alright, I'll tell you all about it. Over dinner."

"Dinner?"

"Yes," Alex says. "Since my show is on hiatus, and I have nothing to do at night."

"Alright, a business dinner. I don't think it's right for me to date somebody involved in a case."

They both laugh. Hammond knows his job is to protect and serve, but to find out who's calling Alex and stalking her, the young detective feels he should lower his guard.

"What time do you want me to pick you up?"

"I'm more of a homebody. I like to cook. All you have to do is bring the wine."

"Alright. I'll be there at 7."

Hammond hangs up and thinks to himself what he was going through. He knows he must find out everything about Dr. Alexandria Birney before she becomes the stalker's victim.

Chapter 7

At police headquarters, Hammond goes to the tech-lab, to ask if they've learned anything new from the caller's fax to Maxine. The answer remains the same as with the rest of the case: nothing. Disappointed, Hammond heads back to his desk. He examines all the clues and knows that without Dr. Birney's help, it'll go nowhere. Captain Railsback talks to his troubled colleague.

"I can see you're in trouble, Boyce."

"I am, Captain. I feel like I'm going nowhere in this case. I don't have a single lead."

Captain Railsback has a simple suggestion, "Let it go."

"What?"

"Let it go for a while. Make him think we failed."

"I can't let him kill Alex, Captain," Hammond replies. "Every second ticking away makes her more vulnerable."

"I understand, Boyce, but right now, we don't have enough evidence."

"We will find the evidence. All I need is a little more time."

"Unless we know who's behind these threats, our time is running out."

"I'll find out who's behind them," Hammond replies, "when I talk to Alex tonight."

"What do you mean tonight?" Railsback asks. "Do you have a date with her?"

Hammond gives his supervisor a devilish smile. Railsback protests.

"Look, I don't believe dating your client is a good idea."

"I understand, Captain, but if we don't find out who's stalking Alex, he'll find her and kill her."

Railsback gives his detective a warning.

"Don't force her to ask any hard questions; I don't want her to be frightened. Remember, it's not only my butt on the line."

"I know, sir. My butt is on the line too."

Hammond needs the dinner 'date' with Alex to shed some light on who wants her dead.

***

Two hours later, at Dr. Birney's apartment, the young doctor starts cooking dinner. She wanted to make sure her dinner will be perfect. Alex hears a knock on the door and gets concerned. She thinks her obsessed caller may have found out where she lives. She grabs a cast-iron skillet from the kitchen and walks up to the door.

"Who is it?"

"It's Detective Hammond. May I come in?"

Alex breathes a sigh of relief; she opens the door as fast as she can. Boyce Hammond is standing at the door.

"As requested, I brought the wine."

Alex smiles, "Please come in."

As Hammond enters her apartment, he guesses Alex's reaction to his knock at the door.

"You mistook me for your stalker."

"What makes you say that?"

Hammond laughs, "The way you're holding the skillet like a tennis racquet."

Alex looks at the skillet in her right hand. "Oh, I'm sorry."

"That's okay, did you ever play tennis in high school or college?"

"Not really, I play racquetball when I'm stressed out."

Hammond feels for Alex. The whole case is one big disaster after another. If the obsessed caller isn't found, it'll be a crushing blow to both of them, especially for Alex. She starts crying and hugs Hammond.

"I'm sick of this, Boyce. I want the nightmares to end right now."

"It's alright, Alex. I'm here to help you, but I need your help. You need to tell me if you know who is doing this."

"I can't."

"Can't or won't? Alex, you've got to help me. If you don't tell me, you won't be safe."

"It's been so long, I can't remember."

As Alex cries on Hammond's shoulder, the oven timer goes off.

"Oh, no. I have to get the scalloped potatoes out before they burn," she sniffs.

Alex heads back to the kitchen and rescues the scalloped potatoes; they've turned out to be perfectly brown. She asks Hammond for help to fix dinner.

"Could you toss the salad? I'm trying to turn over the chicken."

As Hammond obliges, Alex goes to the drawer looking for a corkscrew.

She says. "I thought a cop like you wouldn't be able to get a fine bottle of wine like this on your salary."

"I've always been conservative with handling money," Hammond replies. "I don't think I'd ever get this on a cop salary."

"Is that why you became a detective?"

"That's not even half of it, doctor."

The two laughed as they set up the table. Hammond says the blessing. As they eat, the two avoid mentioning a single word on the obsessed caller.

***

An hour later, Alex and Hammond sat on the couch, listening to smooth jazz music on Alex's stereo and sipping their wine. Hammond has only one thing on his mind.

"Tell me more about Tecumseh."

"Are you talking about the Indian, Boyce?"

"No," Boyce laughs, "I'm talking about where you used to live."

Alex doesn't really want to talk about her hometown. She thinks it would be a boring conversation for Hammond.

"Why are you interested in my hometown?"

"I'm curious."

Alex gives Hammond the truth about Tecumseh, Michigan.

"It's a quiet town, about eight thousand people live there, including my family and friends."

"It seems like a nice, small community," Hammond says. "Do you have a movie theater?"

"There's a cineplex in Adrian; I go there often in the summer or when I see my family during the holidays."

"What else do you do in the summer?"

"On summers, my family has a beach house near Manitou Beach; my father likes to fish around Devil's Lake."

"Devil's Lake? That can't be a real lake."

"Oh, yes. I'm not sure why it's called Devil's Lake," Alex says, "Maybe it's more of an urban legend."

Hammond rebutted, "Why not go fishing near Lake Erie?"

"My father does fish on Lake Erie from time to time, mostly when we go to Sandusky. It's not as convenient."

Hammond's cell phone rings as the two listen to music on Alex's stereo. He picks it up to answer.

"Hello."

It's Maxine on the other line, and she has never been this angry before. Hammond tries everything to calm her down. "Maxine, I can't understand anything when you're shouting."

Maxine explains to Hammond that somebody entered her office and tore up the place. Hammond understands what she said.

"I'll get right on it."

He later contacted the police to bring a squad car over to Alex's house on the double. Alex becomes concerned with what's going on.

"Boyce, what's wrong with Maxine?"

"Someone vandalized her office," he answers. "I'm going down to the station to check it out. I want you to stay in your apartment and lock the doors. Don't let anybody in."

"Boyce, I want to go with you."

"Alex, no. That's exactly what your obsessed caller wants you to do."

As Hammond grabs his gun, he has one more piece of advice for Alex.

"Promise me you'll lock your doors and stay in here until I get back. Please, for me."

Alex nodded. As Hammond leaves, she locks the front door. She quietly sheds a tear, which trickles down her left cheek. She believes that if her caller got into Maxine's office, her apartment might be next on his list.

Chapter 8

Moments later, Detective Hammond arrives with Officer Winter at KPDC. Maxine Hathaway's mood is foul as an obscene comic.

"It's about time you got here, you poor excuse for a flatfoot! I've waited a half- hour for you to show up."

"Would you mind if you keep the noise down," Hammond says, "I've got a headache."

Hammond's head suddenly feels as if it's been kicked around by a world-class soccer team. Maxine's temper is making Hammond's headache even worse. Maxine smells the wine on Hammond's breath.

"My God, Detective," she says. "Are you drunk?"

Officer Winter decides to change the subject.

"Ma'am, could you explain how the incident took place?"

Maxine is furious with the young officer, she takes them to her office and shows them the room with papers and file folders spread around the floor like a hurricane came in and destroyed it.

"I'm thinking about firing the security chief for not stopping the creep who did this."

"Where is your security chief?" Hammond asks, "perhaps he may have a video of who did it."

Suddenly, a man stumbles in, holding the back of his head in pain as he falls on the floor. Hammond and Winter help him into a chair.

Maxine asks, "What happened? Why are you hurt?"

The security chief explains, "I was getting a soda out of the vending machine, and as I grabbed the can, somebody hit me on the head and I passed out."

Hammond is hopeful. "Did you get a look at the attacker's face?"

"No, sir, by the time I came to, I was in the broom closet."

Maxine asks, "How long were you in the closet?"

"About 30 minutes."

"Enough time to trash the place," Maxine says. "Why would somebody go to all this trouble to take out a guard just to trash my office?"

A thought came to Hammond.

"Oh, no. Alex!"

He spots a folder on the floor, and it reads, 'Birney, Dr. Alexandria.' Hammond opens the file folder and sees it empty. He turns to Maxine to ask her a question.

"Did this file contain Dr. Birney's contact information?"

Maxine is still in shock. It hadn't occur to her that the person who trashed her office might be the one who is looking for Alex.

"I can't believe he would do that," she says, "I will never forgive myself if Alex's dies."

Next, Officer Winter comes in with a man who's tied up, wearing only his underwear.

"Detective, I spotted this man down the hall."

"Who are you?" asks the detective.

"I'm the maintenance worker. Some idiot hit me over the head and took my clothes."

Hammond says, "Our culprit must have taken the janitor's uniform to get into Maxine's office."

Hammond and Winter head towards the door. Maxine stands there, preventing them from leaving.

"Where do you think you're going?" She asks. "What about my office?"

Hammond answers, "If we don't stop the stalker before he reaches Alex's apartment, you're going to have one less disc jockey. Oh, and I'll put you in jail for interfering in a police investigation."

Maxine stepped aside as Hammond & Winter heads outside and get in the police car. Winter gets on the CB, telling anyone close to Alex's apartment to head over. Hammond grabs his cell phone to get in touch with Alex.

**

Meanwhile, Alex stands in her apartment, watching the Clock and hoping Hammond will return momentarily. She hears the phone ring and picks it up immediately.

"Hello."

Hammond quickly explains to Alex.

"Alex, it's Boyce. Do you have your doors locked?"

"Yes," she says, "Is something wrong?"

"Whatever you do, do not answer your door."

"Why are you saying this?"

"Your stalker came into the station and trashed Maxine's office. He's heading for your apartment."

Alex panics. She now knows that she isn't safe. Hammond continues to talk to her.

"I already sent a couple of cops to your apartment. We'll make sure you'll be safe. I'll be there in a few minutes. Promise me that you won't open the door until I get there."

"I won't."

"I'll see you then."

"Okay, bye."

After she hangs up the phone, Alex sits on her couch, keeping quiet. Totally unaware that a man has stepped out from his car and is heading towards her apartment. He's wearing a brown suede jacket and a black baseball cap, hoping nobody will recognize his face in the shadow from the brim. He finds the door where the young psychologist is anxiously waiting. He then hears the sound of sirens approaching from the East, getting louder by the second. The stranger retreats to his car and speeds off. The police noticed a speeding car with a Michigan license plate on the back and quickly goes after it.

Hammond arrives as fast as he can. He sees the other squad car going after the suspect thought it was somebody going on a crazed joyride. He heads to Alex's apartment with a gun in his hand and knocks on the door.

"Alex, it's Boyce, could you open the door please?"

Alex opens the door and hugs him. Hammond asked if Alex is all right.

"I'm okay," she says. "When I first heard the sirens, I'd hope they would scare off whoever is coming after me."

Officer Winter is outside looking for clues left when Alex's mysterious stalker took off. He shines his flashlight around the area, and he sees a bouquet of black roses with a card attached to it. He goes to Hammond and reveals what the stalker left. The card is addressed to Alex. Alex opened the envelope and read the card aloud.

Alex:

I waited a long time looking for you. Now I'm here to finish what I started.

Alex Birney is confused and in shock. She doesn't know that her stalker has found out where she lives and will stop at nothing to have her. She sheds a tear as Hammond comforts her.

"Alex, I need to know who might be stalking you?" He asks. "If we don't know who he is, he'll kill you. Who is he?"

Alex finally breaks down. "I can't believe he's found me," she cries. "I can't believe he's the one who called the station and harasses me."

Hammond spots the picture of Alex with the guy whose head is torn off. He puts two and two together.

"Alex, the guy in the picture. Is he the one stalking you?"

Alex won't answer Hammond's question. He continues to ask her.

"Was he your boyfriend?"

Alex looks right into Hammond's eyes and tells him the truth.

"Yes. I can't believe he found me."

Alex cries on Hammond's shoulder; she knows now her ex-boyfriend came down from Michigan to find her. Hammond knows he must protect Alex before it's too late.

Chapter 9

The next day, Dr. Alexandria Birney is at the police station as Detective Boyce Hammond asks her questions in the interrogation room.

"Okay, Alex. The first thing I want you to tell me is this. What was his name?"

Alex takes a sip of water and relents.

"His name is Bronson Metger. He was my boyfriend when I went to Tecumseh High School."

"How long did you two dated?"

"About two years. When I first met him, I thought he was charming. My mom thought he was the perfect gentleman."

"What did your father think of him?"

"At first, he thought he's more like him until he wanted me as his own."

Captain Railsback monitors the interview through a one-way mirror. He's impressed with Hammond talking to Alex about her relationship with Bronson Metger. Railsback keeps quiet as Hammond continued the interview.

"Alex, how did Bronson react when you were going to Michigan State?"

Alex answers, "He didn't take the news too well."

"What did you mean?"

"On the day I got accepted to Michigan State, he tried to make sure I never make it there."

"Would you care to explain to me why he didn't want you to go to East Lansing?"

Alex takes a deep breath and dives in.

***

"It all started when I graduated from high school. My parents planned a small graduation party for me, and a small group of family and friends came over. My father is brilliant at making barbecues. He can make a great rack of baby back ribs, chicken, brats, burgers you name it he'll grill it.

I was getting a diet soda out of the cooler when Bronson showed up. He brought me a bouquet of red roses as a graduation present; they were lovely. I wanted to tell him about my acceptance to Michigan State. He wanted to give me more than roses.

Our conversation was something like: 'I want to talk to you in private, Alex,' he said, 'Is there any way we can go someplace quiet?'

'I don't think it's the right time to tell you something.'

'What you have to say can wait, but what I have to tell you is important. I need to talk to you alone.'

'I'm with my family. Can it wait until tomorrow?'

'No, this can't wait. I need to talk to you now.'

My father came to my aid.

'Is there a problem, kids?'

Before I could answer, Bronson interrupted: 'Oh, no, Mr. Birney. No problem at all. I'm about to give my graduation present to your daughter.'

'Have fun, you two.'

'Oh, we will, Mr. Birney.'

Bronson took me by my hand as we went inside. My brother, Corky, was playing video games in the living room. Bronson wanted some privacy.

'Hey, squirt, your sister and I need some alone time.'

Corky says, 'I'm in the middle of my game.'

'I said leave. Go grab a burger from your father.'

Corky wasn't happy with Bronson forcing him out, but he made sure he got the last word.

'Hey, Alex. I thought you'd dump the creep since you're going to Michigan State this fall.'

I didn't know if Bronson was more furious at Corky for spilling the beans or at me for not telling him. Corky left the house, and we were alone. Bronson wasn't happy with my decision.

'What does he mean you're going to Michigan State?'

I tried to explain, but he wouldn't allow me to speak.

'Why didn't you tell me about it?' He asks. 'Don't you want me to be a part of your life?'

'I do, but I want to focus on my future.'

Bronson had a clear vision of our so-called future.

'You don't need to go to college. Your future is to be my wife.'

He got down on one knee and proposes.

'Alexandria Birney, will you marry me?'

I was in shock, but I knew what I had to do.

'Are you crazy! I'm too young to get married.'

As I tried to leave, Bronson grabbed my arm like a rabid dog that wouldn't let go.

'You can't leave until I get the correct answer. Will you marry me?'

There was only one answer.

'NO!'

'What did you say to me?'

'I said, NO! I am not going to marry you and wouldn't even if you were the last man in Tecumseh.'

As I struggle to break free from Bronson's grip, Corky came back and saw what was going on.

'Hey, you! Leave my sister alone!'

My brother took taekwondo lessons and kicked Bronson in the elbow. The pain caused Bronson to let me go.

'You stupid little brat!'

As I ran out of the house to get my father, Bronson grabbed Corky by the arm and punched him in the face.

'Take that, Mr. Kung Fu!'

Bronson got a real surprise when my Uncle Dave showed up. My uncle was an off-duty cop with the Tecumseh Police.

'What is the meaning of this?'

He looked at Corky on the ground, holding his nose.

'Corky, are you alright, son?'

'I'm fine, Uncle Dave,' he said as blood dripped down from his nose and into his hand. 'I think he broke my nose.'

'Alex, go help your brother. I call the Department.'

I took Corky to the bathroom and told him I was proud of him for standing up for me. We heard the siren of a nearby police car approaching. They asked us questions about what Bronson did and also how he broke Corky's nose. My dad listened as I told the police what happened. He wasn't happy when he heard about Bronson's proposal. I also told him how Bronson grabbed me and punched Corky. The police charged Bronson with assault and battery on a minor. My parents took my brother to the hospital."

***

Detective Hammond asks, "Did you request a restraining order against Mr. Metger?"

"Yes, I did," Alex says. "I thought the nightmare would be over once I filed it. I also thought my experience at Michigan State would be easy."

"It wasn't?"

"No. I never expected to see Bronson's face during my Sophomore year in Lansing."

***

"I was gathering books for Dr. Plensdorf's psychology midterm. I had so many books to carry that they blocked my vision, and I bumped into my psychology professor.

'Dr. Plensdorf, I am so sorry I didn't see you.'

'I say, the way you take teachers to the ground, you oughta try out for the football team.'

I helped pick her up as she helped me get the books.

'I'm sorry, Professor,' I said. 'Are you alright?'

'I'm fine, Miss Barney.'

'It's Birney, Alexandria Birney. I'm considering a major in psychology.'

My decision took Dr. Plensdorf by surprise.

'I'm glad to hear that, Miss Birney. Have you talked to your advisor about it?'

'Not yet, but I will.'

I was heading to my dorm room when Bronson pulled up in a black sports car. He had a bouquet of red roses.

'Hello again, Ms. College Student. Amazingly, you can find someone on GPS.'

I was not happy.

'I told you to stay away from me, Bronson,' I replied. 'I have a restraining order against you.'

'That's nothing but a piece of paper,' Metger said, 'after it expires.'

'Impossible. A restraining order lasts up to five years.'

'Yeah, but with some good behavior from my stint in the klink. I have a clean slate.'

'You're full of it. I'll get my father to call my uncle and prove you're making it all up.'

As Bronson moved towards me, I felt like my flesh was crawling away from my body.

'C'mon, Alex, all I want is to say hello.'

'Get away from me, Bronson. I mean it.'

'Alex, please talk to me for a while.'

'I have a mid-term to study for.'

'Studying can wait, I need to talk to you. I love you.'

'You call busting Corky's nose love? I call it assault and battery.'

'I'm sorry, but he needed to keep his nose out of our relationship.'

'Newsflash, Bronson! We no longer have a relationship. Please leave!'

A campus cop spotted me and came to my rescue.

'Is there a problem, Miss?'

I answered, 'There is...'

Bronson interrupted, 'There's no problem, officer. I used to date her a long time ago, and I wanted to say hi.'

'I don't think bothering our students is a friendly way of saying hello,' the officer said. 'Do you have a visitor's pass?'

Bronson said, 'Why do I need something like that?'

'You need it when you're visiting our campus, sir,' the officer replied. 'Please show me your pass.'

Professor Plensdorf, who also saw what happened, called Lansing police. An officer approached me, asking if there's any trouble.

'Miss, did you call for us?'

'I didn't, officer.'

My professor explained the situation, 'Officer, I called you to help my student. She has been in a terrible relationship, and that man is harassing her.'

Bronson rebutted, 'That's not true, officer. I just wanted to talk to my old girlfriend.'

I told the officer I had a restraining order against him, but Bronson said it had expired. Either way, I didn't want to be near him. The officer had a way of settling the matter.

'May I see your license, sir?'

'First, the mall cop wants my pass, and you want my license,' Bronson said. 'I'm telling all of you I've done nothing wrong.'

'Please show me your driver's license now,' the officer replied. 'If you don't, we will charge you for vagrancy.'

I said, 'Officer, would you please check to see if the restraining order is still intact?'

'Will do, Miss.'

The officer got into his car and scanned Bronson's license. There he found out he wasn't lying about the restraining order being lifted. He also found out he violated his probation for carrying a bottle of OxyContin in his car. The police officer got out of his car to give me the bad news.

'I'm sorry, Miss,' he said. 'According to Michigan law, the restraining order expired over a year ago.'

Bronson was happy to hear the news.

'Yes!! Thank you, officer!'

The officer bursts his bubble.

'There's also some bad news for you, Mr. Metger. I'm afraid you have to come with us.'

'I said, I've done nothing wrong, officer.'

'You call violating your probation no big deal? You're under arrest.'

The officer slapped the cuffs on my estranged boyfriend. When he was placed in the squad car, he said one last thing.

'You can't run from me, Alex. I'll be back, and I'll find you again. Wherever you go, I'll find you!'

That was the last time I ever saw Bronson Metger."

***

"He must have been possessive back when he was with you," Hammond says. "Did you reissue the restraining order after the fiasco?"

Alex doesn't hesitate to answer. "Yes, I did. I kept filing order after order until I left Michigan."

"So, Metger waited until all the orders in Michigan expired," Hammond says. "When you first came here, did you ever think he would try to find you out here?"

"No, I didn't," Alex replies. "I thought the nightmare would be over when I came to California. It turns out I'm wrong."

"And you believe your ex-boyfriend is in San Dimas looking for you and will stop at nothing to find you."

"Bronson found me in East Lansing, Boyce," Alex says. "He'll find me again if we don't stop him."

Alex cries as Hammond consoles her. Hammond makes a solemn vow to his client.

"Alex, I swear I'll find Bronson Metger. And when I do, I'll make sure I'll send him to a cell so dark and dismal he would sell his soul to get out."

Captain Railsback enters the interrogation room. He needs to talk to his detective.

"Hammond, I'm sorry to barge in, but I need to talk to you in private."

Hammond answers, "I'll be right there, Captain."

Before Hammond talks to his supervisor, Alex shows him an old high school yearbook she'd brought with her. It was bookmarked on a certain page.

"What is this?" he asks.

"It's my high school yearbook," she replies. "I thought you might need a picture of Bronson; maybe this could help."

"This could work. I'll send this to the tech lab to see if they could show what he looks like now."

As Hammond gets ready to leave, he asks Alex one more question. "While I'm out. Would you like me to grab a cup of coffee for you?"

"Yes, please," Alex replies. "I take cream and sugar on mine."

"Sounds good."

Hammond leaves the room. Railsback is eager to hear what Hammond learned in his interview with Alex.

"You found out who's our stalker?"

"Sure did, Captain," Hammond says. "Alex told me their story, then gave me her yearbook. We need an age progression photo of Bronson Metger."

"I'll get the tech boys right on it. I also have info on the car with the Michigan license plate."

"Did you contact the Michigan DMV?"

"We did. The car was stolen three months ago."

Hammond asks, "Who's the owner of the car?"

The Captain answers, "It belonged to an orthodontist in Adrian."

"Alex told me about Adrian. I need to contact her uncle in Tecumseh."

"In the meantime, you may have to get some info from Lansing."

"I'm on it. For the last few days, Bronson Metger has been two or three steps ahead of us. This time, we're the ones with the upper hand."

"What about your client, Boyce," Railsback says. "If Bronson sends her black roses to her apartment, he'll try to come back again."

Hammond knows Alex is in a delicate situation. She knows it's Bronson Metger, he knows where she lives, and she knows he will strike again.

"Is there a hotel close to where Alex works?" He asks his Captain.

"Yes, there is, I'll contact them and get someone to keep an eye on her."

"While you do that, I promised to get her a cup of coffee."

Hammond returns to the interrogation room, bringing Alex her cup of coffee. He explains to her what would happen next.

"All I can say is that you helped bust the door down on your stalker."

"Thank you," said Alex. "What's going to happen next?"

Hammond gives Alex a step-by-step explanation.

"From the yearbook you gave me, we're running an age progression photo of Bronson," he says. "By that time, we'll have every station looking for that slimeball. In the meantime, I'm going to put you in a hotel for a few days."

Alex interrupts, "A few days? Why can't I go back to my apartment?"

"You can go back for your clothes, and whatever else you need," Hammond replies. "You're going to have round-the-clock security with you at all times. Where you go, they'll be there with you."

"If they go with me, I can't even go to the bathroom."

"I don't think they'll follow you to the bathroom, Doctor," Hammond says. "We know Metger is terrorizing you, he won't stop until he finds you or does worse."

Alex has only had one regret in her life.

"I shouldn't have come to California; I wanted to start a new life. Now Bronson has followed me, and he's going to kill me, anyway."

Hammond looks at his client, and gives her a hug and a solemn vow.

"Please listen to me, Alex. I swear I will find Bronson Metger, and I'll make sure he'll be in a cell so deep, he would sell his soul to get out."

Alex cries on Boyce's shoulder, hoping he will be the one who could bring Bronson Metger to justice. And he will stop at nothing to make sure Bronson will never stalk Alex Birney again. With the photo she brought in, he knows he has a good start.

Chapter 10

Thanks to Dr. Alex Birney for bringing her yearbook, Boyce Hammond is now looking for the whereabouts of Bronson Metger. Steve, a member of the tech lab, heads to Hammond's desk with some news that'll help with the case.

"Detective Hammond, I have the age progression photo you requested."

"Thank you, Steve," Hammond replies as he looks at Metger's before and after photo. He contacts the man who arrested Metger first. He goes on the internet to find the phone number of the Tecumseh Police Department.

About two thousand two hundred miles away from San Dimas, California lies the peaceful town of Tecumseh, Michigan, where their police department expects a phone call.

"Tecumseh Police Department, Officer Riley speaking. May I help you?"

Hammond answers, "Yes, I like to speak to David Cutler, please?"

"One moment please, I'll get Chief Cutler to talk to you, Mr..."

"Hammond, Boyce Hammond. I'm a detective with the San Dimas Police Department in California."

"One moment, please."

Officer Riley spots Police Chief David Cutler walking out of his office. She tells him about Hammond's call.

"Chief, you need to talk to this guy. He said he's from California."

"California?" The chief says, "Is this a joke?"

"I don't think so," Riley says, "by the tone of his voice, I think it's urgent."

"It better be, for your sake. I'll take the call in my office."

Chief Cutler returns to his office to answer his phone. He's hopes that it's not a practical joke.

"Chief Cutler speaking."

Hammond explains the situation.

"Chief Cutler, you don't know me, but I'm working on a case that involves your niece."

"Alex! Is she alright?"

"She is, sir. She's in a hotel room for the time being."

"What is going on with my niece, Mr..."

"Hammond, sir. Detective Boyce Hammond with the San Dimas Police Department. I want to talk to you about a man you placed in jail seven years ago, Bronson Metger."

The Chief couldn't believe what the young detective said.

"Every time I hear that name, I keep thinking they should put him longer than any sentence the judge can throw."

"Chief, I apologize," Hammond says, "Alex told me what happened at her graduation party."

"There's no need for an apology, son," The Chief replies, "It's Metger's parents that you need to apologize. They had to pay Corky's hospital bills out of his trust fund."

"Chief, I'm faxing you an age progression photo of Bronson. I wonder if he looks like he is right now."

Hammond faxes the photo of Metger to Chief Cutler. As the chief got the photo, he found a previous mugshot of the culprit. The results are incredible.

"Hammond, I don't know who did the photo of Metger, but they did an impressive job," The Chief says with a smile. "It almost looked like his last mugshot photo three months ago."

"Do you have his most recent mugshot, so we can get a comparison?"

"No problem, son. I'll also bring more info about him from our department, and the Sheriff's Office in Adrian."

"What about Lansing?"

"Of course."

The chief wants to ask the young detective a simple question.

"How did Metger find his way of going to San Dimas?"

"I'm not sure how he got here, Chief," Hammond says. "We found a car with Michigan license plates. It belongs to an orthodontist in Adrian."

Chief Cutler has one simple answer.

"My guess is when the restraining order expires, he took the car and headed off where Alex lives."

"He's probably living in a cheap motel near the city limits," Hammond says. "Where he's staying is another mystery."

"Hammond, you're beginning to act like a detective. I'll send the recent mugshot and his records. I hope they will help you, son."

"For our sake, and Alex's, I hope they're more than enough. Thank you."

"You're welcome. You'll have Metger's records as soon as possible."

"Thank you, Chief. Take care."

As Hammond gets off the phone, he receives a fax of Metger's mugshot from Tecumseh Police. Hammond looks at the photo alongside the progressive yearbook picture. The result, an almost perfect likeness. He shows the mugshot to Captain Railsback, and with his permission, they printed a wanted poster. Bronson Metger will soon realize his days of stalking his former high school sweetheart will come in serious heartbreak.

***

Within hours, hundreds of Bronson Metger's wanted poster gets plastered all over the San Dimas area. Supermarkets, gas stations, beaches, and anywhere where citizens try to make a living have a sign asking the public if they saw Metger. All the people reply with a no. Maniac Mike spread the word throughout KPDC's airwaves.

"This is Maniac Mike with a KPDC special bulletin. The San Dimas Police Department is asking for your help in the search for Bronson Metger. He is the man who terrorized this station, and our esteemed colleague Dr. Alexandria Birney and her late-night talk show, 'Midnight Confessions.' He was last seen driving a late-model sedan with a Michigan license plate number DPC-1977. If you see him, please contact the San Dimas Police Department. Callers can remain anonymous, and there is a cash reward for the whereabouts and his arrest. We now return to your regularly scheduled program."

From Maniac's broadcast, the town of San Dimas called Hammond, looking for Metger's whereabouts. Most of them call wanting a piece of the reward money. Hammond knows Metger is out there somewhere in San Dimas, and he needs to find him before he goes after Alex.

***

As Hammond continues looking for Metger, Dr. Alex Birney continues to concentrate more on her occupation. A lone guard stands at the lobby, hoping Metger wouldn't show up. One of her clients asked why there's a cop in the lobby. Alex explains that he's here on police business.

She sees her first client, and she doesn't believe how he sounds.

"Craig, I'm surprised you sound normal than the last time when we talked on the phone."

"I have done what you said, doc," Craig says with a smile. "I have a new job making furniture, so I'm no longer working in the morgue."

"What's the experience like?"

"Like a bad horror movie. I kept thinking a dead body would rise from the slab."

Alex thought of Craig's other job.

"No, I'm talking about your new job. How is it going?"

"It's going great; I'm learning how to build the frames for couches, beds, love seats, you name it."

"Has your new job helped you with your personal life?"

"You mean dating?"

"Yes."

"I haven't found a serious girlfriend yet, but I talk more to people. I'm not as nervous as I first called you. I wanted to say thank you for everything."

"You're so welcome, Craig," the good doctor says. "Please go to the receptionist to set your next appointment."

As Alex takes care of her patient, she sits in her chair and starts worrying. She knows Metger is lurking around, and he'll stop at nothing, whether it's a piece of paper that tells him to keep away from her or a detective who's hunting him in the obvious game of cat and mouse. Alex hears a knock on the door; she opens to see Officer Lovell, the detective in charge of protecting on Alex.

"Are you ready to go, Dr. Birney?"

"I will in a few minutes. I'm feeling like a queen from a third-world nation with you around."

"It goes with the territory, Doctor," he replied, "Detective Hammond wants you to be safe until we bring your stalker to justice."

"I hope he finds Bronson quick," Alex says. "If not, you might have to fix a moat around the hotel, and surround it with crocodiles."

"Don't worry, with everybody keeping their sights on Metger; we'll make sure he won't stalk you again."

Alex and her bodyguard exit her office and head to the parking lot. She noticed on her way to the elevator she forgot her cell phone. They went back to her office to retrieve her cell phone. As they head back to the elevator, Alex has not said a word as they reach the ground floor. Once the psychologist and her bodyguard headed outside for Alex's car, Alex could not believe what she saw. Her car windows are broken by excessive force, and the words 'you're mine!' painted on the doors of her car. Alex couldn't believe the horror of what Metger did to her car. Detective Lovell contacts Hammond to report to Alex's place of work. Hammond knows Metger will stop at nothing to get Alex, and as she sees it, Bronson Metger has her attention.

Chapter 11

Moments later, Detective Hammond arrives at the parking lot where Bronson Metger destroyed Alex's car. Detective Lovell explains the damage.

"When we got to the parking lot, somebody smashed the windows, and painted 'You're mine!' on the doors."

"Metger must've been here," Hammond replies. "Alex was lucky; she stopped to get her phone."

"I'm glad to see we didn't get to her car first," Lovell says, "I mean, she could've been killed."

Hammond spots Alex on her cell phone, making a call to her parents. She tells them she's alright and tells them about Metger running around San Dimas. Mrs. Birney thinks Alex should come back to Tecumseh for a few days. Alex doesn't think so. When she first moved there, Alex wanted to prove she could make it on her own. For the last few years, she successfully did that through private practice as well as her call-in show. With Bronson Metger making threats to her own life, Alex Birney is left without an option. Detective Hammond comes to console her.

"Are you alright, Alex?"

"I'm alright, Boyce. I'm glad I'm not hurt," Alex says, "Bronson will pay for destroying my car."

"If you didn't stop to get your cell phone, he could've done more than trash your car. You could've been killed."

"He didn't kill me, Boyce. He wants me to be as miserable as he is."

Alex starts shedding a tear leading down to her face. Hammond consoles her as best he could.

"Who were you talking to on the phone?" he asks. "I know it's none of my business."

"It's okay, I was talking to my mother," Alex replies. "I told her what was going on."

"What did she insist?"

"She thinks I should come back home to Tecumseh."

"I believe you should listen to your mother."

Alex couldn't believe what Hammond said. She worked so hard to get to where she's going and doesn't want to put everything on hold because of a psychotic ex-boyfriend stalking her like a cat to a mouse.

"Boyce, I can't leave. I have patients to talk to, and I also have a seminar to lecture in college."

"You're in great danger, Alex. I'm saying this as a friend. If you don't take a few days off, your nightmare will get the best of you and Metger will win."

"If I go back to Tecumseh, Metger will follow me again. I need to stay in San Dimas."

Hammond is caught in a consequential dilemma. He wants Alex to be safe from Metger's stalking, but if she goes home, Metger will follow her again.

"Look, I'm going to talk to my captain about you staying in San Dimas with more security for a few days," he says. "If Metger continues to threaten you, you must leave town for a while until we put him in jail."

"I have nobody here, Boyce. No family or friends to help me."

"You're wrong, Dr. Birney. You have a friend here. I'll make sure you won't be another statistic."

Alex hugs her protector. Hammond tells her it'll be alright, like a parent would say to a scared child. His problem now is explaining his idea to Captain Railsback when he returns to the precinct.

***

"That's out of the question. I won't allow my detectives to get involved with the lives of their clients."

Captain Railsback gives a stern lecture to Hammond and Alex back at the precinct.

"Captain, she has nobody here. No family, no friends, nothing," Hammond says, "All she has is her work. Somebody needs to keep Metger here while she's still in San Dimas."

Railsback turns to Alex and asks her to leave the office as he talks to Hammond alone. Alex knew what he'd say to Hammond would not be pretty.

"Boyce, I know you care about her, but keep in mind she's a client."

"I understand, sir. I don't want to see her dead."

"I understand, Boyce, but she's not safe while Metger's on the loose," Railsback says as he hears the phone ring. "Now I have to answer the phone."

Railsback picks up the phone.

"Railsback here. Yes, Detective Hammond is with me. I'll hand the phone over to him."

Railsback hands the phone over to Hammond like a baton to a relay runner.

"Hammond, here."

The person calls from the Snowball's Chance Motel, near the San Dimas city limits. She has something about Metger, which she wants to tell the detective.

"Let me get this straight, ma'am. You're saying the suspect we're looking for is staying in your motel."

Hammond continues to listen to the caller's explanation. She mentions the stolen car with the Michigan license plate. It's spotted outside the parking lot.

"I'll be right over. Bye."

As Hammond hangs up the phone, he asks his captain for a request.

"I like to have two warrants, Captain."

"Two warrants?"

"One, an arrest warrant for Bronson Metger."

"And the other?"

"A search warrant, sir. We could find out how Metger is threatening Dr. Birney."

Railsback smiles, "Now you're a detective. Get the warrants; I'll get Detective Lovell to take Dr. Birney back to her hotel room and add extra security."

Hammond thanks Captain Railsback as he leaves his office. Railsback stays in his chair and notices one thing.

"I forgot to tell him not to date his client. Oh, well."

***

After he gets the warrants, Hammond goes to the Snowball's Chance Motel. An old run-of-the-mill Motel on the outskirts of San Dimas. As Hammond gets there, he spotted the stolen car with the Michigan license plate in the parking lot, a perfect match. All of a sudden, he hears a familiar voice he heard over the phone.

"Excuse me," the stranger says, "are you with the police?"

"Yes, ma'am. My name is Boyce Hammond. I'm a detective," he says as he shows the stranger his badge. "Are you the one who called?"

"Yes, I'm Maria. I called you about Mr. Metger."

"I have a search warrant, do you know where Mr. Metger is staying?"

"You bet. I'll show you where he's staying."

Hammond and the motel manager arrive in the front lobby to find out what room Metger's staying. They recognized he's staying in room 13.

Hammond asks, "Do you have a spare key?"

Maria answers, "Are you kidding? I have more keys than a piano."

Maria grabs the spare key to Metger's room.

"Besides, the cheapskate owes me two days for staying the night."

Hammond arrives at room 13. He gives Metger an ultimatum.

"Bronson Metger, this is the San Dimas Police Department. Come out with your hands up. You are under arrest."

There's no response from inside room 13. Hammond gives Metger one last warning.

"I'm ordering you to come out, Metger. If you don't, I'll come in."

The room is still silent. Metger wouldn't answer to Hammond's last warning.

"That's it, Metger! I'm going in!"

Hammond takes the key and opens the door nice and slow. He didn't see Metger but was surprised to see a lot of things found in his room. He sees a collage of photographs of Alex from her days in high school. Old articles of Alex from various newspapers during high school and college. And an ad for Dr. Birney's radio show. Hammond knew he had found the honeypot when he spotted a few electronic devices like a laptop which Metger used to contact the station. It is an enormous piece of evidence against Metger. Hammond calls the precinct.

"Captain, this is Boyce. I'm at Snowball's Chance Motel. I'm in the room where Metger is staying."

Hammond checks the bathroom and sees the window was open. Metger already made his escape, and Hammond heads out the door to stop him. By the time he gets to the door, his suspect had gotten away. Hammond contacts his supervisor.

"The bad news is Metger got away. The good news is I found plenty of evidence which the tech boys can look at."

Railsback contacts the tech lab to meet with Hammond. As Hammond leaves room 13, he already knows his suspect has a good head start. When he gets to his car, he sees all four of his tires had been slashed by a knife, complements of Metger. Boyce Hammond is in a really foul mood by cursing up a storm. He picks up his cell phone and contacts Railsback one more time.

"Captain, it's me again. When you send the tech boys over, you better call a wildcat."

Railsback asked his young detective why he needed a wildcat sent. Hammond gives his explanation.

"Metger slashed all four of my tires. He's got a big head start while I'm stuck in the middle of a heatwave!"

Hammond waits in the lobby until help arrives. Ironically, the only chance he has in catching Bronson Metger and bringing him to justice is the same as the name on the motel, a snowball's chance down below.

Chapter 12

It's been two hours since Hammond is left stranded outside the Snowball's Chance Motel as Bronson Metger slashed all four of his tires. He waited for a wildcat to come and tow his car. Hammond got a ride back with the boys from the tech lab after they collected all the evidence from Metger's room. When he gets back to the precinct, he doesn't want to talk to anybody about what happened. Captain Railsback tells Hammond to come to his office. As Hammond enters his supervisor's office, Railsback knows his top detective is in a foul mood.

"I want to kill Bronson Metger!" Hammond says. "I want to strangle the punk with my bare hands!"

"First of all, calm down!" Railsback says. "I know you want to kill Metger for what he did to your car, but when you're in my office, I need you to calm down."

Hammond catches his breath as he calms down. "I'm sorry, Captain. I am ticked off. All four of my tires are flat because of him, and he's out there somewhere laughing at us."

"He got away, but remember, we got all the stuff he has in his room."

Hammond wonders, "Have we got any more info about Metger?"

Railsback pauses for a moment to give his reply.

"It's why I asked you to come here."

Railsback gives his young detective a series of envelopes. Each of them involving Metger's arrests. Railsback also gives Hammond a phone number.

Hammond asks, "Where did this come from?"

"Adrian, Michigan. Compliments of the Lenawee County Sheriff's Department," Railsback replies, "Sheriff Hennegan is eager to speak with you."

"I'll get right on it, sir."

Hammond leaves the captain's office and hopes he might get more info on Metger. He heads back to his desk and gazes at the phone number, thinking about calling the Sheriff. Instead, he looks at the envelopes sent from the police stations in Tecumseh and East Lansing. According to those stations, Metger's police record was a mile long. Charges include assault, harassment, stalking, and holding up a couple of convenience stores. Hammond also found something which could shake the core of the case from the Lenawee County Correctional Facility. He opens the envelope and sees one thing he couldn't imagine about Metger; his college grades from prison. Hammond becomes confused with Metger's transcripts; he contacts the Lenawee County Sheriff's Department to look for answers. Deputy John Willet picks up the phone.

"Sheriff's office, Deputy Willet speaking."

Hammond answers, "Yes, I like to speak to the Sheriff, please."

"Who is this?"

"I'm Boyce Hammond; I'm a detective with the San Dimas Police Department in California. My Captain gave me this phone number to talk to him."

Deputy Willet spots Sheriff Leroy Hennegan leaving his office; Willet tries to stop him.

"Sheriff, I have somebody on line 1 who needs to talk to you."

Hennegan replies, "I'm heading for home. I can't talk to him now."

"The call is from California, Sheriff," Willet says. "I don't think this could wait."

Hennegan forgot about contacting the cops investigating the Metger case out west.

"I'll take it in my office, Willet."

Hennegan goes back to his office and picks up the phone.

"Sheriff Hennegan speaking."

Hammond talks to the sheriff.

"Sheriff Hennegan, my name is Boyce Hammond. I'm from the San Dimas Police Department."

"Of course, I talked to your captain earlier today. I heard you had some car trouble."

"I don't want to talk about it, sir. Especially with that punk on the loose."

"My apologies, son, I don't joke around with guys who remind me of Bronson. I understand how you are feeling."

"Thank you, sir," Hammond says as he picks up Metger's transcript. "One thing got me confused, though."

"Oh, what would that be, Detective?"

"This college transcript from the prison; I never thought Metger could be smart."

"You need to talk to Warden Johnson about it."

"I didn't know prisoners can get an education from behind bars."

"They can do that, Mr. Hammond. They could even try to get a job once they pay their debts to society."

"I guess it's true, the hardest part of getting out of prison walls it's finding themselves back in society."

"It's also why I wanted to explain to you, Mr. Hammond," the sheriff says. "Bronson Metger escaped from prison two months ago."

"What!"

Sheriff Hennegan explains, "After he got his degree, he hacked into the prison's mainframe. Once he did that, he stole the car and headed to where your client is living now."

"I want to know how Metger would find info on Alex."

"He might have paid somebody to find her."

"There are a lot of private investigators around the Greater Los Angeles area, Sheriff," Hammond says, "I would be humiliated if I got hired by a criminal."

Hennegan agrees, "If he has experience with hacking into computers, he must have a way to find Dr. Birney."

Hammond asks the sheriff another question, "We also encountered the car Mr. Metger stole from the Michigan DMV. Have you contacted the owner of the car?"

"He died of a heart attack when he headed to his car."

"How did it happen?"

Hennegan explains, "Our deputies found the body of the orthodontist where his car stood."

"Don't tell me."

"Yes, he died once we took him to the hospital."

Hammond feels like he got sucker-punched in the gut by an unranked heavyweight contender. Metger proves he can kill somebody to get to Dr. Birney, and he'll be sure that he'll do it again. The only person who stands in his way is Boyce Hammond.

"Detective Hammond," the sheriff says, "are you alright? You seem so concerned."

"Sheriff, I am concerned," Hammond says, "I need to stop Bronson Metger from putting another innocent life in jeopardy."

"Well, son, I wish you the best of luck on this one," Hennegan says, "I hope you find him, so we can extradite him to Michigan for first-degree murder."

"I won't promise you, Sheriff. I'll try to do that."

"Let's hope so, for our sake and Dr. Birney's. Take care, Detective."

"You too, Sheriff. Goodbye."

After Hammond hangs up the phone, he hears it ring. He thought it was Alex who's now worried about him. He picks up the phone and says.

"Hi, Alex."

An unpleasant voice is heard on the other line.

"Guess again, honeybunch," the caller says with a laugh.

"Metger! I should have known you have the nerve to call me for real."

"Oh, I'm crushed. You try to look for me at the motel and take my computer and my electronics as I slashed your tires."

"What do you want, Metger?"

"You know what I want," Metger says. "I want my girlfriend back."

"What part of it's over, don't you understand?" Hammond replies. "Alex is happy now, and you can't let her be happy. You are pathetic!"

"Who's more pathetic, Hammond? Me, or her knight in shining armor sitting in his desk waiting for my next move?"

"You listen here, you wasted sperm-and-egger. I am going to find you, and I am going to stop you from threatening Alex again."

"Good luck, hero. When you try to look for me, it'll be too late."

Metger laughs over the phone as Hammond listens in disgust. He hangs up the phone in the mood that's unaccepted. He calms down for a few seconds and called Alex to give her the news. Alex is in the shower of her hotel room; her voicemail tells him to leave a message. Hammond gives his message.

"Alex, it's Boyce. I hope you're alright. If you get this, please call me at the station. It's important. Thank you. Bye."

After leaving Alex a message, Hammond hears another ring. This time it's Alex after she got out of the shower.

"Did you call me, Boyce?"

"I did, Alex. I thought you must have gotten another call from Metger."

Alex says in a sarcastic tone, "Why would I ever get a call from Bronson?"

"Because he's nuts! I had a conversation with him over the phone a few minutes ago."

Alex is in shock; she knows now if Metger finds her, the consequences will be disastrous. Hammond wants to talk to Alex in private.

"Alex, is there a way we should talk about this privately?"

Alex is thinking the same thing.

"I was thinking the same thing if there is no trouble?"

"No, Alex. No trouble whatsoever."

"I thought of dinner tonight, just the two of us. I'm thinking of something fancy."

Hammond interrupts, "You know how Captain Railsback would say. I'm not off duty yet."

"Please, Boyce. You told me you'd protect me no matter what."

"I have, I made a vow to do that. I won't stop until Metger is behind bars, and en route to Michigan."

"To Michigan? What for?"

"Murder, and Grand Theft Auto. I'll explain it over dinner."

"Okay then, will 7:30 be alright?"

"7:30 will be fine."

"I'll see you then, Boyce. Bye-bye."

"Bye."

After Hammond hangs up the phone, he puts his hands on his head and thinks about why he is putting up with this case. He thought the case was taking a toll on his mind more than his body. All Hammond can do is continue hoping, hoping that Bronson Metger shouldn't get to Alex Birney first.

Chapter 13

A few hours later, Detective Boyce Hammond heads off to the hotel where Dr. Alex Birney is staying. As he heads to the top floor, his mind is still on Bronson Metger, and wondering when that piece of slime will strike next. The elevator stopped and opened its doors as Hammond steps out. He walks into the hallway where he sees Detective Lovell on guard duty.

"Good evening, Boyce. I'll tell Dr. Birney you're here."

"Thanks, Reed. I'll be waiting."

A couple of minutes past and Alex walks out the door in a slinky red cocktail dress and matching high heels. Detectives Hammond and Lovell couldn't believe their own eyes.

Lovell says, "I think I need to date a shrink."

Hammond replies, "Sorry, Reed, she's already taken."

Alex looks at Hammond and asks, "Are you ready?"

Hammond says to his date, "Ready as I'll ever be."

The two walked down the hallway and into the elevator as it goes down to the ground floor. They both act quietly as the elevator heads down. Hammond looks at Alex, and he never thought she could be sexy.

"I never thought of you dress like that," Hammond says. "I thought of you as conservative, not drop-dead gorgeous."

"Oh, this little thing, I have had this since I graduated from Michigan State," Alex says. "One time, it got me out of a speeding ticket in Okemos."

"Where on Earth is Okemos?"

"Near Lansing."

Hammond couldn't believe what Alex said. The elevator doors opened as the two stepped out. Alex doesn't know Hammond was going to take her on a night on the town in a squad car.

"Boyce," she says, "this is extremely different."

"It's a loner until I get the tires on my car put in," Hammond replies. "Metger is going to pay for that."

As the couple gets in the police car, Alex had one more question to ask.

"Are we gonna be on active duty if we get a call?"

"I don't think so, besides it's hard to go on a date with a couple of criminals in the back."

The two drove down to the Red Rose, as they head towards the entrance, a valet wanted to place the squad car in a parking space. Hammond tells Alex to step out while he puts it in a parking spot. Once Hammond parks his car, he turns the keys over to the valet.

"That was fast," Alex says, "I thought he would get it to park."

Hammond replies, "I don't like the idea of him joyriding. Shall we dine?"

"Let's."

The two go to the restaurant and get to their table as soon as possible. The waiter arrives with a couple of menus for them. Hammond opens his menu, unaware he is reading it upside down. Alex giggles to herself on Hammond's mishap.

The waiter asks the couple, "Do you two want something to drink?"

"I'll have water," Hammond says.

"I'll also have water," Alex says.

The waiter replies, "Very well, then. I'll be back with your drinks and your appetizers."

The waiter leaves as the two decide on what to eat. Hammond stared at what is on the menu, and some items are difficult to pronounce.

"I can't understand what's written on the menu."

Alex offers to help the detective out, "Let me look at your menu."

Alex looks at Boyce's menu, and she recognizes what language it's written.

"It's French," she says, "I took French in high school and college."

"I also think you studied in France when you went to college, right?"

"I wanted to go, but I didn't have the money for the trip. I even got a job during school, and I still couldn't go."

"Because you didn't have the money, Alex?"

"No, my boss at the time had me working non-stop, and I never got the chance to study abroad."

"Alex, you're a therapist now, you can afford to go on trips like Paris."

"I do, but I don't have the time to go on vacation, especially with that maniac on the loose."

Alex cries after what she said. Hammond goes to console her.

"Alex, it's okay. I'm here. We'll stop Metger, and when we do, I'll make sure he'll never bother you again."

"What happens if you don't find him?"

"We got the entire Los Angeles County looking for him, Alex," Hammond replies. "He can run, but he can't hide for long. Believe me, when I say this to you, we will get him. After he's gone, you can take a long vacation to anywhere you want."

"I thought about the shores of Saint-Tropez. Maybe somewhere in the Virgin Islands, anyplace would be perfect for getting out of here."

Alex cries on Hammond's shoulder. The waiter asks Hammond if everything is alright. Hammond tells him everything is okay.

The waiter says, "I'll come back in a few minutes to take your orders."

Hammond nods as the waiter lets them be. Alex heads to the ladies' room to freshen up. Hammond goes back to his chair and finishes his drink. He worries about Alex after what menacing nightmare she's going through. He also worries about Metger. Boyce knows he's still around San Dimas on the run from the police and trying to make Alex's life miserable. Alex comes back to her table as Hammond offers her a chair. She's impressed with what he did.

"I've seen nobody pull out a chair for me. You didn't do this cause you feel sorry for me."

"No, I wanted to be a gentleman."

"Thank you."

"You're welcome. I hope you can help me translate the menu."

Alex couldn't believe what Hammond said. She knows it's not his fault; it's his first time being at a fancy establishment without a drive-thru window.

"Don't worry about the check, Boyce. I'll take care of it."

"I thought it was the man who would pay for dinner."

"Yes, but at these prices, I don't think you can handle what they cost."

Alex looks at what Hammond can't decide on because he has trouble reading an unfamiliar language.

"I think you'll like the prime rib, Boyce."

"Prime rib? I can't afford that on my salary."

"Try to keep it down, Boyce. Besides, this is on me. I wanted to do this because I care."

Hammond talks to his client in a quiet tone.

"It's nice of you to think about it, but I don't think it's right to get involved with someone I'm working with. Whether it would be my colleagues in the police department or with my clients."

Alex understands what Hammond said.

"You're right, Boyce. I'm sorry, I want to do something nice for you helping me in the last few weeks. I hope I can get my radio career back on track."

"Alex, it will happen. Metger can't hide forever, and once he's caught, your career will blast off. Maybe they'll recognize you on a national level."

"Boyce, it's sweet of you to think about it," Alex says. "I don't think I'm ready to go national. I want to get noticed in San Dimas first."

"Okay, let's start with San Dimas, then work on California, and then we go National."

Alex laughs at Hammond's idea, but she thinks he might have a point. She thought if Midnight Confessions did well, other stations might air it. Until Bronson Metger is in the deepest, darkest cell they can find, her dream will never take flight. The two enjoy their dinner, and their conversation.

***

After their dinner, the young detective takes the psychologist back to her hotel room. The two giggled as the elevator goes up to the penthouse. Alex and Boyce gets out of the elevator to notice Detective Lovell dead.

Alex screams as she sees Lovell's body on the floor. Hammond sees the door to Alex's hotel room busted open. Hammond contacts the police on his phone, reporting a code blue. He then takes out his gun as she tells Alex to stay where she is. He goes to the room and sees that it's ransacked. On the walls, Hammond sees a message posted in Lovell's blood that reads:

I'LL FIND YOU!!!

Metger is hot on Alex's trail after finding out where she lives, and now knowing where she's staying, he'll stop at nothing to get his hands on Dr. Birney. Boyce Hammond knows somebody is giving Metger information to where Alex Birney is hiding, and he needs to find the deranged sicko before he kills Dr. Birney or anybody else who gets in his way.

Chapter 14

As the coroner takes Detective Lovell's dead body to the morgue, Captain Railsback discusses with Detective Hammond in the ransacked hotel room of Dr. Alex Birney.

"This is a real nightmare," Railsback says. "The first question I want to ask you is, why did you take Dr. Birney out for a date without me knowing about it?"

"It wasn't my idea, Captain," Hammond says. "She doesn't like the idea of playing the role of a princess while the hotel room acts as a tower, and Bronson Metger plays the role of a dragon."

"So, you want to play the dragon slayer, right?"

"I might be the one to do it, so yeah."

Railsback has other plans in mind for this fairy tale.

"This is no fairy tale, Hammond. Metger is scarier than a dragon, a witch, or any other thing that's evil in any kind of storybook."

Alex overheard the conversation between Hammond and Railsback. She had a set of luggage with her. Hammond attempts to stop her.

"Where do you think you're going?"

"I'm going to the airport and head home to Tecumseh," she says. "I don't want to be a burden for anybody."

Captain Railsback agrees with Alex's decision, Hammond doesn't.

"Captain, please give me another chance," he says, "I believe I can get Metger before he gets her."

"Boyce, if you want to stop Metger, you need to keep Dr. Birney out of harm's way," the captain says. "Besides, heading back home to Michigan would be perfect for the good doctor."

"And if she goes back to Tecumseh, Metger will follow her."

Alex throws in her two cents.

"Don't I have an opinion on this?"

Both Hammond and Railsback had a simple answer.

"No!"

Hammond has one more suggestion.

"I don't think your dress would be appropriate to head to the airport."

Alex says, "I have a pair of jeans and a sweatshirt in my duffel bag."

"Put them on," Hammond says. "Metger wouldn't recognize you if you're incognito."

Railsback couldn't believe what his top detective said.

"Now, you're starting to think like a detective, Hammond."

Hammond sees one of the lab technicians wearing a baseball cap. The young detective has an idea.

"Hey, I got a question to ask you."

The technician says, "What would it be, detective?"

"Is your baseball cap adjustable? I believe she needs it."

"It's my good luck cap; I can't get rid of it."

"It would be a lot of good luck with my client."

The technician refuses to give up his lucky cap. Alex has an idea of making him give up his prized possession.

"How about I give you money for your cap?"

"How much would you want for it?"

Alex goes to her purse and takes out some money.

"Would fifty dollars cover it?"

Hammond doesn't agree with Alex offering a bribe.

"Alex, what are you doing?"

"You want me to go incognito, Boyce. I'm offering a chance to do that."

The technician says, "Forget it; I had this when I first started."

Alex calls the technician's bluff and antes up.

"I'll give you a hundred dollars for it."

"I still can't get rid of it. It's not for sale."

Railsback lays down the law on the technician.

"Now you listen to me, mister. We have a psychopath who killed one of our officers," he says as he points to Alex. "This girl is in great danger, and her stalker doesn't get her, but he will again. So if you don't accept her money for your baseball cap, you're going to deal with worse luck than she is. Got it!"

The technician hands Alex his lucky baseball cap. Alex gives the technician her money.

"I'll bring it back once the case is over."

"Keep it; I have a couple more caps like that."

Alex doesn't like the idea of being played by the technician.

"That dirty snake," she shouts to Hammond, "he conned me a hundred dollars for this cap."

Hammond plays the role of a peacemaker.

"Let it go, Alex. You need to get out of San Dimas before Metger finds you. Let's go to the airport."

Alex leaves with Hammond to go to the airport incognito and out of a hundred dollars.

***

Moments later, Detective Hammond takes Dr. Alexandria Birney to the airport. In her mind, the young psychologist doesn't want to go back to Tecumseh, not with Bronson Metger on the loose. Hammond doesn't like the idea either, but he took an oath to protect and serve. He also thought it's for the best, hoping she'd be out of town to keep Metger at bay in San Dimas. As they wait for Alex's plane that will take her to Detroit, Alex begins to have second thoughts on the whole ordeal.

"I think this is a mistake," she says. "I shouldn't leave while Bronson is still looking for me."

"I agree with you one hundred percent, Alex," Hammond replies, "but Captain Railsback disagrees with us. Which is why you need to go home and let me deal with Metger."

Alex is sad because she wants Metger to get the justice that's coming to him in spades. Hammond knows if Alex stays, she will get in the way with his case.

"Alex, I know you want to see Metger get what he deserves," he says. "Let me take care of it. The sooner you get on that plane, the easier for me to keep him at bay. What Metger doesn't know won't hurt you."

"That's what I'm afraid of, Boyce," Alex replies. "If I go, he'll find me back in Michigan."

"He won't find you while he's still in San Dimas. I'll make sure he doesn't leave."

Alex sheds a tear as the intercom issues the last call for her flight to Detroit. Hammond gives her a kiss, knowing everything will be alright. He gives her one last demand.

"Please, get on the plane. For me."

Alex goes to the gate to fly back to Detroit. Hammond could only watch seeing her go.

***

Outside the airport, Hammond watches the plane which carries Dr. Alex Birney take off as it heads for Detroit on her way back home to Tecumseh. As the plane leaves the dark skies of Los Angeles, Hammond drives back to San Dimas, alone. He heads to the parking lot of the San Dimas Police Department about to tell his supervisor Alex is heading home. But first, he gazed over the city, knowing that Bronson Metger is still around.

"If you're looking for Alex, Metger, you're too late," he says. "She's on the next plane out to Detroit, on her way back home. All those years, you've stalked her, thinking she's your property. Let me tell you one thing, a car can be your property, a house can be your property, but a human being. A human being is not your property."

Hammond continues to look over the city, knowing Metger hears every word he said.

"All you do is hide," he continues, "hide with all your fancy high-tech gizmos and do hickeys. Knowing somebody like Alex would be scared, and you take advantage of her at her weakest. I'm here to protect Alex as I serve you the biggest humiliation you'll get. I'll leave you in a bloody mess that your family can't identify you at the morgue."

There is still silence across the city, silent enough for Hammond to scream.

"Where are you, Metger? You're not tough now, you little maggot! It's your turn to be the victim, make your move, Bronson! What are you waiting for!"

Officer Schneider couldn't help but hear Hammond shouting to the heavens.

"Are you all right, Detective?" He asks.

Hammond answers, "I'm okay. I had to take Alex to the airport. I'm going to talk to Railsback and call it a night."

"Okay, goodnight, Boyce."

"Goodnight, George."

Hammond heads to the station, telling Railsback that Alex is on her way home. He later called it a night. As he got home, he slept on the couch, upset. Because Alex is somewhere in America at 30,000 feet while he's at home dealing with her psychotic stalker. As he tried to lie down, Hammond realizes one thing. Somebody is feeding Alex's information to Metger.

Chapter 15

The next morning, Detective Hammond returns to the San Dimas Police Department, depressed and hurt. He couldn't sleep over the fact Alex got on the plane last night, hoping she'd be alright. Captain Railsback looks at his top detective and knows how miserable he was after last night.

"Good morning, Captain," Hammond says.

Railsback replies, "You look like crap, Boyce."

"I feel like crap, Captain," exclaimed Hammond. "I couldn't sleep after what happened yesterday."

"It's only to help Alex while we capture her slimeball stalker."

"If he doesn't know, she's headed back home."

"What do you mean, Hammond?"

Hammond sits down and gives his explanation to his supervisor.

"As I returned from the airport, I had a bizarre premonition on how Metger knew where to find Alex."

"You mean how he knows where she's living in that apartment or staying in the hotel."

"Even where she works," Hammond says, "I believe somebody paid off Metger to where he might find Alex."

Hammond's theory has got his supervisor concerned about what he said.

"What do you mean by that?"

"Somebody gave Metger information on where Alex lives, works, or even where she stayed in the hotel."

"You mean somebody is helping Metger find Alex?"

"Somebody close to Alex is giving Metger the information, sir."

As Hammond explains his theory to Railsback, they both hear the phone ring. Railsback picks the call up.

"Railsback speaking."

The caller asks for Hammond and to place the call on the speaker. Railsback turns on the speaker as the detectives overhear the conversation.

"Hello, Hammond, I know you're in your boss's office."

Hammond couldn't believe what he heard. The caller sounded like Bronson Metger when he called the station.

"Metger!" he shouted. "You can't talk like that; we got all your electronics and do-hickeys."

"All but one, Detective, and I'm using this to talk to you."

"I don't know how you got this number, but I've got somebody tracing this call..."

Hammond is unaware of some snickering in the back.

"Who's that giggling!" Hammond shouted.

The caller starts talking in his normal voice; it was Vincent behind the strange voice asking for both Hammond and Railsback to come to the tech lab.

***

As the detectives head to the tech lab, Hammond grabs Vincent by his lab coat and pins him to the wall. Hammond is not in a funny mood.

"You think it's really cute what you pulled today," Hammond says, "but I'm not in a good mood."

Railsback maintains order between his detective and his technician.

"Boyce, let him go," he says, "he's not good to us dead."

Hammond releases the technician.

"Now, apologize to him," said the Captain.

Boyce replies, "He should apologize to me first."

The technician asks, "Don't I have anything to say here?"

Hammond and Railsback both replied, "NO!"

The technician wants to plead his case, "Boyce, I'm sorry about the phone call. I thought you might find it funny."

Hammond wasn't in a cheerful mood, "I don't find it funny. Pulling something stupid like you did can put somebody's life in danger, maybe your own."

Vincent replies, "We would never pull something like what we did. We try to get to know how this thing works."

Vincent shows the detective and his supervisor the laptop.

"The laptop you found can also help with the voice changer."

Hammond asks, "How can he do that?"

Vincent explains, "First, Metger contacts his callers and records the conversation, and once he has a sample of their voice. He would use an app on his phone to help change his voice."

Vincent uses his cell phone to prove his theory. The phone rings from the tech lab. Hammond picks it up.

"Hello."

Vincent was on the other line completing his hypothesis.

"While Metger speaks in his voice on his phone, the other caller hears an unfamiliar voice from the actual speaker."

Strangely, the technician is talking in Alex's voice. Hammond is one part shocked, and the other part unhappy as he leaves the lab. Vincent had a concerned look on his face.

"What's eating him?" He asks the Captain.

Railsback is in a furious mood as he explains to his top technician.

"I'll tell you what's eating Hammond," he says. "He had to see his client leave town on an airplane flight to Detroit while her crazed ex-boyfriend is stalking her around this city."

The Captain also looked at the gizmos on the table.

"Not to mention the little stunt you pulled made him upset."

"I wanted to help you and Detective Hammond with the case," Vincent says. "I would do nothing to harm him."

"You would be the one explaining to him once I calm him down," The Captain replies. "I wouldn't want to be in Hammond's shoes if I were you."

The Captain leaves the Tech Lab for a moment to see Hammond with his head hung low. He knows his top detective couldn't handle the fact Alex is already in Michigan while the technician plays the role of a bad stand-up comic attempting to go for the punchline.

"Boyce, I know how you're feeling," said Railsback, "I need to ask you this question, what would Dr. Birney do in your situation?"

Hammond raises his head and gives his supervisor his answer.

"She would've followed orders and hope we would capture Bronson Metger here instead of having him go back and stalk her in Michigan."

"Indeed. I know it was hard for you last night, but you said before we got here, you thought Metger is getting help from somebody."

"Yes, I did, Captain. Who's helping him is a different answer."

Railsback replies, "Perhaps the lab boys have it on the computer."

Hammond heads back to the lab. Vincent issues an apology to the young detective.

"Detective Hammond, I want to apologize for my actions. I do not intend to make fun of your problem."

"I accept your apology, Vincent," Hammond replies. "Right now, we have a criminal to stop. Is there anything you found on Metger's laptop?"

"Other than the different voice tracks, you better believe it."

Vincent shows Hammond something extra on Metger's laptop.

"We went through the laptop and got a call log from one of the files."

"A call log?" Railsback says in confusion. "I thought you found those on your cell phone."

"You do, Captain, but with the way Metger designed it, he would use his computer to act as a cell phone."

Hammond says, "It's the same way they do video calls or chats."

Vincent replies, "Yes, but not the way Metger does it."

Vincent also shows Hammond and Railsback another clue from the laptop.

"I also found a number which Metger use a lot during his time in the Snowball's Chance Motel."

Hammond gazes at the phone number seen on each line repeatedly.

"Do you have the person who has the number?"

Vincent answers, "I thought you never asked."

The technician types in the phone number, and Hammond is in for a big surprise. Once he saw whose phone number it was, the young detective's blood ran cold. The number belongs to Maxine Hathaway, station manager of KPDC radio. Vincent saw a worried look on Hammond's face.

"Are you alright, detective?"

Hammond turns to the lab technician and says, "No, but I am gonna solve this case."

Hammond walks out of the tech lab, gets to his car with a warrant in his hand, and heads off to the radio station to talk to Maxine Hathaway.

***

Ten minutes later, Hammond heads to KPDC radio. He walks to the door like Hannibal invaded Rome without a herd of elephants charging in.

The receptionist asks, "Can I help you?"

Hammond replies, "No, thanks, I'll find my way here."

The receptionist blocks the elevator, "Look; I can't let you walk in to speak to Ms. Hathaway."

"I think you should step aside while I talk to your boss."

"Sir, she's in a meeting."

"I have a warrant that says she will answer me. Please, step aside before I arrest you."

The receptionist steps aside as Hammond gets in the elevator. As the door closes, she had one thing to say.

"I'm going to call security."

Hammond rebuts, "While you're at it, call the Marines."

The door closes as the elevator goes up to the top floor. As it stops, Hammond exits and heads for Hathaway's office. Hathaway's secretary tries to stop him.

"Sir, you can't see Ms. Hathaway, she's in a meeting."

"She'll answer to me," Hammond says as he enters Maxine's office.

Once inside, Hammond sees the only person who's in the meeting is Maxine Hathaway herself.

"You better have a good explanation of why you interrupted this meeting, or I will tell your Captain to suspend you!"

Hammond gives Maxine a simple question, "Why did you sell Dr. Birney to a psychopathic stalker?"

"That is not the point!"

"It is the point! The boys at the tech lab found a call log in Metger's computer with your phone number."

Maxine couldn't believe what Hammond said.

"What you are saying is a bunch of fake news," she says. "I can't be the one who betrays my on-air staff."

"You did more than betray Alex's trust," Hammond replies, "You tossed her overboard for shark bait."

"You're crazy; I have done nothing to Alex."

"In that case, we can talk about it downtown. You are under arrest."

"You're making a serious mistake, Detective Hammond. I'll have your badge for this."

"Tell it to Metger who doesn't know Alex left," Hammond says as he puts the handcuffs on Maxine.

"What do you think you're doing?"

"I'm doing my job, Ms. Hathaway. I'm going to take you to the station."

"You can't do this to me. I have rights!"

"Of course you have rights, Ms. Hathaway," Hammond replies. "I am going to read them to you. You have the right to remain silent."

Maxine shouted a slew of obscenities as Hammond read her rights. She tells her secretary to contact security. The receptionist came from the elevator with two security officers. They want Hammond to leave the station and to release Maxine. Hammond shows the security officers the warrant issued for Maxine's arrest. The officers couldn't challenge the warrant and let Hammond take Maxine to the precinct. Maxine threatens to fire anyone who doesn't come to her rescue. Hammond knows without Metger's connection; he may force him to surrender if he isn't foolish enough to go after Alex.

Chapter 16

After placing Maxine Hathaway under arrest, Detective Boyce Hammond takes her to the San Dimas Police Department. Maxine has not moved a muscle in the interrogation room. She doesn't say a word as Hammond asked her questions about her relationship with Bronson Metger.

"Alright, Maxine, I'm going to ask you this question," he says. "What's the deal with you and Metger?"

The room is in complete silence. Hammond is not in the mood to get Maxine's silent treatment. Railsback looked at the conversation through a one-way mirror. He isn't happy with the way Maxine refuses to answer any of Hammond's questions. Hammond shows Hathaway the evidence between her and Metger.

"The boys at the tech lab found this call log from Metger's computer," he says. "The majority of his calls are direct to you."

Maxine says in furious anger, "I'm not talking to anybody but my attorney. I'm going to have your badge when I'm through with you."

"Look, we got a woman who's in fear for her life, and you are wasting everybody's time. Tell me, why are you talking with Bronson Metger?"

"That's none of your business, Detective. I won't say anything until my attorney gets here."

The door opens, and a man with a bad suit and a crooked hairpiece comes in.

"Maxine, I got here as fast as I could," he says as he looks at Hammond. "Is this the man who threatened you?"

"First of all, I don't know what hole you crawled out from, but this is police business."

"Everything is my business," said the crooked lawyer, "I'm accusing you of manhandling my client."

Captain Railsback has had enough of the lawyer's shenanigans. He goes into the interrogation room, and gives the lawyer a piece of his mind.

"Now you wait one moment you cheapskate," he says, "What Detective Hammond did was by the book. Your client refused to answer his questions at the radio station, so she will answer his questions right here."

"Your detective interrupted a meeting, Captain."

"The person I saw in her office was Maxine," Hammond answered. "I want to know who you are and why you should be arrested by not only the police but by the fashion police?"

The lawyer says, "Oh, I almost forgot to introduce myself. How stupid of me."

The shyster lawyer hands his business card out to Hammond which reads:

Harold S. Palmer
Attorney-at-Law

"I've seen your type before," Hammond says. "You're the one who gets their law degree from the back of a cereal box."

"Impossible, I earned my degree like everybody else."

"Of course you did," Hammond replies, "you bribe the dean to get it. Isn't it right, Harry Palmer?"

"Stop calling me that," Palmer says, "I oughta sue you right now for slander, and making fun of my name!"

"Enough!" Railsback shouted as he turns to Maxine's lawyer. "Your client refused to cooperate with Mr. Hammond in an investigation he's working on, so he placed her under arrest."

Maxine interrupts, "I'm not the one who's on trial here."

"Oh, really," Hammond replies, "Then why are you aiding and abetting a felon?"

Palmer couldn't believe what Hammond says, Hathaway turns her back afraid of hearing the truth.

"What did you promise Metger in return, Ms. Hathaway?" Hammond asks.

Maxine refuses to answer the question. A silence broke down the room for a few seconds. Hammond goes a little tougher on his line of questioning.

"Did you promise him a job at the station?"

The shyster lawyer says, "My client will not answer any more of your questions, detective."

"She will answer all my questions," Hammond replies, "because she's a co-conspirator."

"A co-conspirator?" Palmer says. "How dare you call my client a co-conspirator when she did nothing wrong?"

"If it involves Alex's life, it involves everything this case stands for," Hammond replies as he stares at Maxine. "I don't think the judge will be happy if you don't tell us the truth."

Palmer has to butt in to protect his client.

"My client has a right not to incriminate herself, Detective," he says, "now if you excuse us, she will pay her bail, and we will leave."

Hammond stops the crooked lawyer dead in his tracks.

"Not so fast, Harry Palmer! Ms. Hathaway's bail is set at $30,000. Unless you have the cash, she's going nowhere."

Hathaway and her lawyer talked amongst themselves, the same thing with Hammond and his supervisor. Railsback thought of one way of Hathaway avoiding jail time.

"Okay, Ms. Hathaway, we decided you can post your bail," he says. "There is one condition you must do for us."

Her lawyer replies, "Forget it; there are no conditions for my client."

"If she cares about not going to jail, she'll help us," Hammond says. "Otherwise, the District Attorney is pretty vicious when it comes to stalker crimes."

"What do you want my client to do, Detective?"

Hammond looks straight into Palmer's eyes and gives the shyster lawyer his response.

"Your client is going to help us place Bronson Metger where he belongs, behind bars."

Palmer gulps at Hammond's proposal. He knows the young detective is serious about helping Alex in every way, and he doesn't care how he wants Metger as long as he doesn't leave town to find and kill Alex.

"What do you want to know?" asked Hathaway.

Hammond replies, "How about we start from the beginning."

Hathaway and her lawyer sit down; she tells Hammond and Railsback about her first encounter with Metger.

"It was three months ago when I first met Bronson," she says. "He was looking for a job at the time. I didn't know he was an ex-con."

"He's an escaped con, Ms. Hathaway," Hammond says, "We found out from the info given to us by the Lenawee County Sheriff's Department."

"Metger is sneaky with his resume," Maxine says, "he listed some jobs he did that I thought were too good to be true."

Hammond gives a simple reply, "He doesn't want his prison status to be a factor."

"I thought Bronson's resume was bogus when I did a complete background check on him."

"Were you right about it?"

"I was," Maxine replies. "It turns out his background was clean."

Railsback thinks it's ridiculous, "There's no way Metger's background check is clean. My detective has Metger's rap sheet from three police stations in Michigan."

Hammond adds, "You have to have an uber genius IQ to make it look spotless, or be pretty darn good with a computer."

As the conversation continues, Officer Tucker interrupts the pow-wow.

"I'm sorry to interrupt," he says, "but Detective Hammond has a phone call."

"I'm in the middle of an interrogation, Kevin," Hammond replies. "Tell him to leave a name and message, and I'll call him back."

"I can't, it's a long-distance call from Michigan," Tucker says. "It's urgent."

Railsback tells Hammond he'll take the call and tells him to continue his interview with Maxine.

"Alright, Maxine. I want to know how you conspire with Metger?"

"Don't answer the question, Ms. Hathaway," Palmer says, "I don't want you to incriminate yourself."

Hammond turns to Maxine's slimy shyster lawyer and says, "If your client wants Dr. Alex Birney alive and well, she needs to answer every question I ask her. Get it!"

Maxine sheds a few tears as the interrogation gets harder and harder for her to answer any of Hammond's questions. She doesn't want to see a tombstone with Dr. Birney's name on it. If she tells Hammond about her connection with Bronson Metger, it would not only betray her trust with Alex but also affect her career.

"I'll talk! I'll talk!" she says to the Detective. "I'll tell you why I'm helping Metger."

Palmer wouldn't allow his client to talk, "No, if you tell him, your life will be in ruins."

Maxine turns to her lawyer, "Better mine than Alex's."

Maxine turns to Hammond and tells the young Detective what's going on.

"He knew about me going to see Alex," she says. "He hacked my cell phone and found out I saw another person."

Hammond says, "You're telling me you're having an affair? Does your husband know about this?"

"Detective Hammond, I'm not married," Maxine replies, "I've been in a relationship with my partner for about four years, and Metger hacked into my cell phone to blackmail the board if my affair goes public."

"So your affair may get you to lose your job as station manager," Hammond says.

"Yes, it would."

Hammond thought of a risky idea, and he hopes Maxine would try to cooperate with him and the police.

"If you help me with this case, and help Dr. Birney," he tells Maxine, "we will dismiss the charges against you."

Maxine answers, "To help Alex and maybe regain her trust. I accept."

Maxine's lawyer protests Hammond's proposal, "I don't think it's your business what you're doing to my client."

"A woman's life is at stake, Harry Palmer," Hammond replies, "that makes it my business."

"What do you want me to do?" Maxine asks.

Hammond replies, "Do you have any info on Metger's phone number?"

"I have to get in touch with the phone company," Maxine says, "I have to get a call log from them."

Hammond replies, "The sooner you get the call log to us, the better. We need to keep Metger at bay while he's still in San Dimas."

"I hope you know what you are doing with my client, Detective," the crooked lawyer says.

"For Alex's sake," Hammond replies, "I hope so."

Hammond lets Maxine post her bail as she and Palmer left the station. As the two go outside leaving police headquarters, Palmer couldn't believe what Maxine was going to do.

"Maxine, I don't think it's right for you to help the police."

Maxine disagrees, "I got Dr. Birney into this mess, and I'm going to help the police stop it."

As she got into the cab, Maxine turns to her lawyer and gives him the only words he would never hear.

"By the way, Harry Palmer. You're fired."

The cab drove off, leaving Harold Palmer all alone. Perhaps he should've let Maxine continue helping the police. He turns to his cell phone and contacts an unknown source for help.

"Listen, I need your help," he says. "My ex-client is going to help the police."

The person on the phone overheard what Palmer said. He tells the crooked lawyer not to worry as he takes care of the problem.

"I know you can take care of my problem," Palmer says, "and don't worry about the Detective. I'll get somebody to stop him. Thank you, Mr. Metger."

As Palmer hangs up, he tries to head for his car. Unaware, it's being towed by a wildcat for parking in a space reserved for police officers only.

***

A few hours later, Maxine Hathaway is at her lavish home. She contacts her phone provider to send her a call log from last month. She hopes finding Bronson Metger's phone number could help the police in tracking Alex's psychotic ex-boyfriend. Suddenly, a shadowy figure sneaks in through the back door by picking the lock. Maxine is still on the phone talking to the phone company, but as she gives them her address on where they can send her the call log. The stranger shot Maxine Hathaway in the back of her head three times as her body falls flat on the floor. The killer picks up the phone and places it back on the base.

The killer goes back the way he came in. As he gets to his car, he takes off his mask, revealing himself to be Bronson Metger. He contacts Harold Palmer that his mission is complete and expects to have his money as soon as possible. He tells the crooked shyster to get rid of Boyce Hammond to get the money.

***

Meanwhile, in his apartment, Boyce Hammond spends the rest of the night tossing and turning in his bed. His phone rings as he keeps dreaming of Alex, knowing she's alright in Tecumseh. Hammond gets up in a state of drowsiness as he picks up the phone.

"Hello," he says as his voice slurs.

"Boyce, I'm sorry I wake you up at this time," said Captain Railsback, "but I need you at Hathaway's house right away."

Boyce doesn't feel like going to Maxine's house in the middle of the night.

"Captain, It's 2 a.m.," he says, "what's the reason for waking me up?"

The Captain gives him the reason why he's needed.

"I'll spell out the reason for you. M-U-R-D-E-R."

Hammond couldn't believe what his boss said. "Did you spell, murder?"

"Yes, I did, Boyce," Railsback replies, "get to Maxine's house right now."

"Okay, I'll go," said Hammond. "Tell me who's the body?"

Railsback gives his top detective the most honest answer he knew.

"Boyce, Maxine Hathaway is dead."

"WHAT!"

"Somebody killed her earlier this evening."

Hammond couldn't believe what he heard. He thought Maxine might help him with his case against Metger; now, he's back to square one.

"Let me get dressed, Captain. I'm on my way."

As Hammond hangs up the phone, his only concern is how far will Bronson Metger go to find Alex Birney, and who will he kill next if they stand in his way.

Chapter 17

After he got dressed, Boyce Hammond arrives at the home of Maxine Hathaway. Police act as peacemakers when reporters try to ask who murdered Maxine. As Hammond goes through the yellow tape, Officer Tim Glaser stops him.

"I'm sorry, sir, but authorized personnel can come in."

Hammond shows Glaser his badge, which causes the young officer to have second thoughts.

"Detective Hammond, I'm sorry I didn't recognize you, sir."

"Apology accepted, Tim," Hammond says as he crosses the tape. "I know you're following orders. Make sure no reporter gets in."

"Will do," said Glaser as he sees a photographer attempting to cross the tape. "Hey, you, the one with the camera. Get back to your side; this is a restricted area."

Hammond couldn't believe how eager Officer Glaser is. He goes inside to the murder scene. He shows his badge to fellow officers as he headed to the location of Maxine's dead body.

"How did Maxine die?" he asks the coroner.

Tina Porter, the coroner, shows Hammond where the station manager died.

"It seems our assassin acted like John Wilkes Booth when Ms. Hathaway was on the phone," she says. "I believe the time of death was about three hours."

"Any explanation on how the killer came in?"

"Lab boys are checking every door and window in the house. My money said he must've gotten in through the backdoor."

While the tech boys look to where the killer got in the house, a technician found a set of footprints in the backyard leading towards an alarm system with all the wires cut. He contacts Hammond on the situation. Within seconds, Hammond goes outside to look at the vandalized alarm.

"Somebody knew how to take out the alarm before he could get in," he says. "A man who knows his way around electronics."

The trail of footprints leads to a back door leading to the kitchen. The technician shines a light on the doorknob where he and Hammond notices one thing. There are scratch marks around the key slot. The technician has a crazy hunch.

"Somebody must've picked the lock."

Hammond thought he was the one being the detective.

"I believe you're learning how to be a detective, Mr..."

"Connors, Jason Connors, sir," said the technician. "I've been working here for six years."

"Okay, Jason. How do you deal with somebody messing with the door?"

Jason thinks of the only answer he knew, "Are there fingerprints on the doorknob?"

"Let's find out."

The technician uses a spray that can detect through ultraviolet light. As he sprays the doorknob, he uses an ultraviolet flashlight to reveal nothing. The two are not happy with the results.

"No, fingerprints," said Jason, "I believe the killer had gloves on when he picked the door."

"I think you're onto something," Hammond says. "Keep looking for more clues; the killer might've left something when he escaped."

"Will do."

Hammond takes another look inside Maxine's mansion. He knows the killer hid in the shadows when he shot Maxine. He asked Officer Baxter if he found more clues from the den.

"Negative," he says to the Detective, "I believe our culprit got away with the perfect murder."

"Impossible," Hammond replies. "No murder can be perfect. The killer must've had something to hide."

Baxter has a simple thought, "What if Ms. Hathaway used the phone the moment she died?"

"The killer would kill her as she was on the phone."

Hammond tells Baxter to contact the phone company for a call log with whom she called before her death. He tells the officer one more thing.

"Call them on your phone. Maxine's phone is now evidence."

"Roger."

Hammond heads outside. A couple of reporters ask him questions on who killed Maxine and what he knows about the case. Hammond has nothing to answer at the moment. He now knows the case involving Alex Birney and Bronson Metger has gone from bad to worse.

***

The next morning, Hammond heads back to KPDC radio, but this time he waited outside to talk to Maniac Mike Martinez. As Maniac heads out the door, he gazes at Hammond, standing in front of his car waiting to talk to him. Maniac has one simple response.

"I'm not the man who murdered Maxine Hathaway," he says. "If I were, I wouldn't be the one reporting her death in the middle of the night."

"I listened to your show last night," Hammond replies. "You may have the nickname of Maniac, but to me, you're harmless."

Maniac takes it as a compliment. He knows having a life outside the radio station differs from being on the air five days a week.

"How are you doing, Detective?" he asks Hammond. "Is there any word from Alex?"

"No, I haven't heard from her," Hammond replies, "but I'm doing alright in a city that's all wrong."

Maniac couldn't agree with him more. He knew since Alex is halfway across the country in the hopes she'd be safe from Bronson Metger.

"It's not much fun without her, Detective."

"I know what you mean, Mike. She's safe until I bring her psychotic ex-boyfriend to justice."

Maniac has a bizarre feeling, which might shed light on the case.

"What if somebody paid Metger to kill Maxine?"

Hammond couldn't believe what the shock jock said. He also believes Metger wouldn't do anything to stoop so low.

"I don't think Metger would go to Maxine's house and kill her," Hammond says. "Even scumbags have morals."

"Not all of them do, Detective," Maniac replies. "It would make my job less easy."

Hammond agrees, but he decides to change the subject.

"What do you think of Maxine's attorney?"

"Are you talking about the guy who dresses like a bad 70s sportscaster with a plaid checkered sport coat and a bad rug with a matching pornstar mustache?"

"Yes! Have you met him?"

"I hate his guts," Maniac replies, "he looked like somebody who would sell clunkers."

"Clunkers?"

"Clunkers, lemons, used cars which should be in the junkyard."

"The ones who couldn't be repaired at all."

"You got it!"

"I had an encounter with him yesterday at the precinct when I interrogated Maxine."

"How did he respond?"

"Like a snake-oil salesman," Hammond answers. "I wasn't interested in buying what he was selling."

The two men laugh, but the shock jock is serious with what he mentioned.

"I'm serious, Detective. What if Metger is the one who killed Maxine?"

"It could be a possibility, but I need to get all the facts first before I bust him for murder."

"When will you get the facts first?"

"Later today, when I talk to that little weasel."

"Do you need backup?"

Hammond turned to Maniac and says, "No, I'm good."

Maniac replies, "Not as much as that shyster is going to be."

The two men laugh and go their separate ways. Maniac goes home to get some sleep while Hammond heads off to talk with Harold S. Palmer: Attorney-at-Law.

***

After talking to Maniac, Detective Hammond arrives at the law offices of Harold S. Palmer. He enters the law firm's door like a bull in a china shop. Palmer's secretary attempts to intervene.

"Sir," she says, "Mr. Palmer is in a meeting."

"Don't worry," Hammond replies, "it's not gonna take long, anyway."

"I'm gonna call the police, sir."

Hammond flashes his badge to Palmer's secretary. He gives her one piece of advice.

"While you're at it, call the National Guard."

Hammond goes to Palmer's office and sees the slimy shyster all alone. The young Detective knows one thing is true.

"Funny, I don't see anybody at the meeting."

Palmer felt as if he soiled himself when he saw Hammond through the door.

"You better have a good explanation why you're here, mister," he says, "because I'm going to contact your Captain and sue you and the police department for harassment."

Hammond dis-confirms, "Harassment means nothing when it involves murder, Harry Palmer."

"Stop calling me Harry Palmer, I hate being called that name," Palmer says as he comes to his senses. "What do you mean, murder?"

"Maxine Hathaway died last night in her home," Hammond replies. "Somebody came into her house and shot her in the back of her head."

Palmer couldn't believe what he heard. The shock from his face figured he would ever conspire with Bronson Metger in Maxine's murder. Like a snake-oil salesman dealing with tons of complaints from his customers, Palmer thinks of a quick lie.

"I didn't know about my ex-client's death, Detective."

"Ex-client?"

"You heard me, ex-client!" Palmer says. "That no-good witch fired me when I told her not to get involved with you in the Metger case."

"I believe you are in some way involved with Maxine's murder," Hammond says, "On the other hand, I may lack the evidence to make sure you get a lawyer who's slimier than you.

Palmer breathes a sigh of relief, thinking he's off the hook. Hammond has a different thought as he gets close to the no-good shyster.

"I will say this to you as an officer of the law," he says with a serious tone. "If you lie to me, I'll be back. With a warrant, and a pair of handcuffs."

Hammond leaves the crooked attorney's office with a determined look on his face. A look which made Palmer cringe. He picks up the phone and calls Bronson Metger secretly.

"That detective has got on my only good nerve," he says. "I want him out of the picture, for good."

Metger says, "Don't worry about it, I'll handle the detective. Remember, we still have a deal."

"Don't worry, I'll find out where your girlfriend is hiding. Get rid of the cop first."

"With pleasure."

As the conversation ends, Palmer places his elbows on his desk and gives a sadistic grin hoping Bronson Metger should stop Boyce Hammond in the hopes he would find Alex Birney no matter what. In Hammond's case, he's heading towards an inescapable trap.

Chapter 18

After dealing with Maxine Hathaway's former lawyer, Detective Boyce Hammond drives back to the San Dimas Police Department. A mysterious car follows him closely. When he got to the red light, the young detective gazes at his rearview mirror and sees the driver tapping his bumper on his black sedan to the bumper on Hammond's car. The driver behind him laughs as Hammond grips the steering wheel tight as the light goes from red to green. Hammond heads off as the car behind him continues to follow. Hammond is still heading back to the precinct, knowing the black sedan is yet suspiciously following him. The young detective uses his CB, hoping if any squad car within a couple of miles has their ears open.

"To any officer hearing my voice, this is Detective Boyce Hammond," he says, "A suspicious man is following me in a black sedan. I may need some back-up."

The mysterious man doesn't want Boyce to get the message out as he bumps into Hammond's car.

"Officer in trouble, I repeat, officer in trouble."

As Hammond requested back-up, the driver goes to another lane and tries to run Hammond off the road. He bumps into the driver's side door. The guy in the black sedan is mad because Hammond is still holding on. Suddenly, the lane the sedan is on is ready to merge right with the flow of traffic. That's when Hammond turns on the siren and tells the driver to pull over. The driver couldn't believe he got played like a violin, but he needs to get away from the law. So he steps on the gas and leads Hammond on a wild chase through San Dimas. Hammond gets on the CB.

"This is Detective Hammond requesting back-up. Chasing late-model black sedan on Huntington Ave. Any unit around the area is requesting back-up."

A police car answered the call, "This is car 18, we're near the area, and we'll be there shortly."

The squad car sees Hammond chasing the black sedan and starts following the chase. The sedan goes faster, but Hammond isn't giving up; he thinks if the guy could drive him off the road, so can he. Hammond goes to the left lane and tells the culprit to pull over. The driver looks at Hammond and gives him the finger. As the speeder laughs, he did not see the other police car in front of him as the car crashes into it. Hammond and the other squad car comes down to check the scene.

"Check to see if anybody is all right," Hammond says.

The officer replies, "On it."

Hammond goes to the driver in the busted sedan and takes out a pair of handcuffs. He gives the driver a simple command.

"Would you mind stepping out of the car, sir?"

The driver gets out of the car as Hammond places the cuffs on him and reads him his rights.

***

After the arrest, Hammond is in the interrogation room talking with the hit-and-run culprit.

"All right, you worthless scumbag," he says, "I want to know who you are, and why you try to run me off the road?"

The culprit spits in Hammond's face. Hammond feels like he wants to take the culprit to the intensive care unit until Captain Railsback asks Hammond to step outside for the moment.

"Captain, I want to take these two hands and wring his neck."

"You do that, and you'll be off the force for police brutality."

"He tried to run me off the road, Captain."

"I know, I know from the report you gave me," Railsback replies, "I believe we have a bigger problem to deal with."

"Captain, I can't deal with a bigger problem than the one I'm interrogating right now."

"We found out who the creep is working for."

"You have," Hammond replies, "I want to know who this John Doe is?"

"We got the info from the license plate on the damaged car."

Railsback gives his young detective the info on his hit-and-run culprit. His name is James Waggoner, an unemployed construction worker. He got fired a week ago for complaining of working overtime when his kids had a little league game. He tried to kill his boss with a rivet gun. Currently, he's out on bail awaiting trial. As Hammond gets ready to continue interrogating Waggoner, he sees a familiar face he doesn't want to see again.

"I believe I should sue you for harassing my clients, Detective."

Hammond couldn't believe the idea of Harold S. Palmer coming in to represent Waggoner.

"What made you come here?" he asks the shyster lawyer. "Did you use the police scanner to know where they're at?"

"That is none of your business where I know where my future clients are," Palmer replies, "it's where they keep them that matters."

Hammond wants to grab the shyster lawyer by his throat. Railsback has a different theory in mind.

"Boyce, let him talk to his client."

Hammond doesn't like the idea, "But Captain, I don't want this slimeball to interfere in my case."

"I know, but Waggoner has the right to an attorney," said the Captain, "and whether we like it, Harry Palmer is his lawyer."

Palmer is in a foul mood, "It's bad enough for you detective to call me that name, but now you have to call me that name?"

"Go talk to your client before I let Hammond arrest you."

Hammond leads the attorney to the interrogation room to go see his client. He asked them if they want anything.

"I'm going to get a cup of coffee," he says. "Would you like a cup?"

"None for me, thank you," Palmer says.

Hammond turns to Waggoner, "Would you like some coffee?"

Waggoner replies, "I like to leave this room, right now."

"I'm afraid it will take a while until you have your bail posted," Hammond replies, "I suggest you both need some coffee."

"I'll have some," said Waggoner.

"Alright then," said Palmer. "I'll have a cup."

124

DAN COLLINS

"I'll be right back," Hammond says as he leaves.

The young detective goes to get the coffee while Railsback tells him to come to the one-way mirror. Hammond keeps quiet as Palmer and Waggoner continue to have their conversation.

"Jeez, I can't believe you would stoop so low to kill a cop," Palmer says. "What on Earth are you thinking?"

"I was told by Bronson Metger to keep the detective out of his hair," Waggoner replies. "Besides, he told me it was your idea."

The crooked lawyer tells his client to be quiet.

"Will you shut up, the cops are listening to what you're saying."

Hammond knows it was nothing but a set-up as he continues listening to the conversation. He wants to go back to the interrogation room and beat those two men up. Railsback has a different strategy in mind. He tells Hammond to keep listening to the conversation to find out what happens.

"I don't think you should talk about Bronson Metger when the detective comes back," Palmer says to his client.

"But he offered me a ton of cash to put that pesky cop-out of commission," Waggoner replies, "I needed the money, it's hard for me to find a job ever since I got fired."

In the other room, Hammond insists on placing Waggoner and his slimeball lawyer in the Intensive Care Unit. Railsback tells his young detective to be patient as they continue listening to the conversation.

"I think I need to get the coffee," Hammond says.

"Our coffee pot is not working," Railsback says, "get it somewhere else."

Hammond has a crazy idea, "I know where I could get some."

Meanwhile, Palmer continues the conversation with Waggoner.

"One more thing, James," he says, "if that no-good detective asks you anything about who paid you to kill him. LIE!"

"What choice do I have," Waggoner replies, "I told my wife I'm looking for a job."

Hammond heads back to the interrogation room with three cups of coffee. Palmer isn't happy with the detective taking his own time.

"It's about time you show up, Hammond," Palmer says, "you need to use GPS to find your way back here."

Hammond played along with Palmer's remarks.

"I'm sorry, but our coffee pot broke down, so I got some from internal affairs."

Hammond gives Waggoner and his lawyer their cups. As the lawyer takes a sip, he spits it out as if his mouth is on fire. He later knocks his cup and spills the remaining coffee on his lap. Palmer is on the floor, screaming in pain.

"Oh, I forgot to tell you, gentlemen," Hammond explains. "The boys at internal affairs like their coffee three ways; strong, black, and scalding hot."

Palmer threw an array of obscenities as he continues to be in excruciating pain. James Waggoner couldn't help but sit and watch the moment happen in front of his own eyes. Hammond looks at Waggoner and tells him what he wants to say.

"Mr. Waggoner, I'm going to say this once," he says. "I want to know where I might find..."

Before Hammond could say Metger's name, Detective Thomas Gage came into the interrogation room.

"Detective Hammond, Detective Hammond. I need to talk to you."

"Not now, Gage," Hammond says, "I'm talking to this slimeball."

"There's a phone call for you in your office."

Hammond is not happy with Gage's interruption. He turns to Waggoner and says.

"I'll deal with you later."

He then turns to Gage. "Place him back in the cage."

Gage looks at Palmer on the floor, cursing up a storm.

"What about him?" he asks Hammond.

Hammond answers, "Call the medics, and tell the boys from internal affairs I said, 'Thank you'."

As he leaves the interrogation room, Hammond heads to his desk to answer whoever's on the phone.

"Detective Hammond here."

A familiar voice is on the line with a concerned tone.

"Hello, Detective Hammond, this is Chief Cutler from the Tecumseh Police Department."

"It's great to hear from you, Chief," Hammond says with a smile. "How may I help you?"

The Chief is not in a good mood when talking to the detective.

"Have you heard from Alex in the last few days?"

"No, sir," Hammond replies, "I thought she's back home in Tecumseh."

"I'm afraid she's not home," said the Chief. "Her mother called me today, wondering where she is."

"I'm sorry, Chief, but I was there when she got on the plane to Detroit."

"I contacted the airport in Detroit," said the Chief, "the plane arrived, but no sign of my niece."

Hammond worries; he knows if Alex is not on the plane, she might be in another part of San Dimas. A ploy that would lure Metger out of hiding to get his attention.

"Chief, I don't know where Alex is," he says. "If she's still in the area, I'll find her before Metger does."

"For your sake and mine, Hammond, I hope you'll find her," The Chief replies. "I hope she won't do what I think she'll do."

"Which is?"

"Find Metger and kill the little punker."

"Don't worry, Chief. I'll find your niece."

"I know you'll find her, Hammond. I hope it won't be too late."

"It won't, Chief, not on my watch. Good day, sir."

"Good day, Detective. Bye-bye."

After Hammond hangs up the phone, Captain Railsback wants to know what is going on with the Metger case.

"Boyce," he says, "is there something you haven't told me?"

"I'm sorry, Captain. I'm not only dealing with a deranged psychotic stalker, but I have to deal with the fact that Alex was not on the plane."

"WHAT!"

"I saw her got on the plane," Hammond says, "she must've left before it took off."

Hammond bangs on his desk with his fist.

"Captain, I feel so stupid."

"Quit blaming yourself, Boyce. You need to find Metger before he finds out Dr. Birney is still in San Dimas."

In Hammond's mind, he knows his supervisor is right. If Bronson Metger knew Alex didn't get on the flight back home, she would be in serious jeopardy. Hammond has one idea when dealing with the deranged psychopath.

"Captain, tell the officer to bring Waggoner back to the interrogation room. I have only one question to ask him."

Railsback asks, "What question would that be, Hammond?"

Hammond stands up and explains the question to his boss.

"I'm going to ask him where I might find Bronson Metger."

Chapter 19

After a long talk with James Waggoner in the interrogation room, Detective Boyce Hammond heads down to where he first met Bronson Metger. Waggoner tells the Detective about a bar called the Wrecking Ball. He says he goes there every time he does construction. After he got fired, Waggoner spent most of his time drinking beer instead of finding a job. Hammond goes to the bartender, asking for information.

"What will it be, Mac?"

"I was going to ask you about somebody," Hammond says as he shows the bartender his badge.

"Look, Mac, whatever you got on me, I didn't do it."

"Relax, I need you to answer a few questions."

"Who sent you?"

"Waggoner, James Waggoner. We got him for reckless driving, and he tried to run me off the road."

The bartender couldn't believe Waggoner would do such a thing.

"Look, I've known James Waggoner for years," he says. "There's no way he could do such a thing."

"It's a bigger problem for someone who lost his job."

"All I know, Detective, is that James would never do such a thing."

"Maybe, but I believe he wasn't alone."

Hammond takes out a photo of Metger.

"I want to know if you've ever seen this man?"

"Not really," said the bartender, "I saw that guy's face plastered all over town."

"Do you know somebody who recognized him?"

Hammond keeps his focus on who knows about Metger spending his time at the bar. A waitress comes forth to tell the detective what happened.

"I believe I know who you're looking for."

Hammond replies, "What do you know about the suspect, Miss...?"

"My name is Amy, Detective," she answers. "I started working here for almost a month."

"How do you know about Bronson Metger?"

"To avoid any foul language," Amy replies, "he's a real scumbag."

Hammond asks, "Are there any examples you can explain?"

"I have a couple of examples, Mr... Oh, I'm sorry, I don't know your name."

"It's Hammond, Detective Boyce Hammond," he replies as he gives Amy his business card.

"When I gave him his beer, he started whistling and cat-calling me," said Amy. "He even slapped my behind."

"What happened after he slapped you?"

"At first, I wanted to take a mug of cold beer and smash it in his face."

"You would have been in jail for assault and battery if you did something like that."

"Look, I'm nobody's baby, nobody's hot mama," Amy says. "I took that mug of cold beer and poured it on his lap. To me, it's a more civilized thing to do."

"Remind me not to get on your nasty side," Hammond says. "What happened after you poured beer on Metger's lap?"

"He cursed up a storm," Amy replies. "He grabbed me by my wrist and wouldn't let me go. Thank God for Zeus to come in and stop him."

"Who is Zeus?"

"Zeus is our head bouncer," Amy replies as she points to Zeus. "Hey, Zeus! Someone wishes to talk to you."

Hammond takes one look at Zeus, and he's staring at a mountain of a man. He stood 6 feet 5 inches tall and weighs close to 280 pounds of solid muscle. Black as the Ace of Spades, his physique casts a shadow over Hammond as he stares at an eclipse.

"Is there a problem?" he asks.

"No problem," Hammond says as he shows the bouncer his badge. "I like to ask you a few questions."

Hammond shows Zeus a picture of Metger.

"Do you recognize this man?"

Zeus notices the picture right away.

"I've seen that guy," he replies. "I've seen guys like this creep almost every day."

"Has Bronson Metger showed up here in the last couple of days?"

"Sure did, he was at the bar hitting on Amy, and wouldn't leave her alone. I tossed the punk out like he was yesterday's garbage."

"How much do you lift?"

"Six hundred pounds, the guy I tossed was a lightweight."

Hammond chuckles at Zeus's remark. He asks the bouncer one more question.

"What did you do before you became a bouncer?"

"I was in Iraq for the past two years," Zeus says. "I got hired after my stint with the Marines."

"I joined the Navy out of high school," Hammond says, "I pulled a tour of duty in Iraq and Afghanistan."

"I can't believe a cop like you is a veteran," Zeus says with a smile. "I took the job as a bouncer to get back in college. I'm planning to run my own business when I graduate."

"I'm happy to hear that, Zeus," Hammond says as he hands his business card to the bouncer. "If you see Bronson Metger anywhere, please call me."

"You got it, from one veteran to another."

Zeus and Hammond shake hands. Hammond feel as if his hand went through a vice as Zeus let go.

"Sorry, I didn't mean to hurt your hand."

"It's okay, Zeus. I only need this hand for my gun. Call me if you see Metger again."

"Will do."

Hammond heads back to Amy; he tells her to call him if Bronson Metger shows his face again. Amy agrees. As he leaves the Wrecking Ball, Hammond hopes Metger will try to come back again. He heads to the nearest pharmacy and bought an ice pack for his right hand, compliments of a bouncer named Zeus.

***

Meanwhile, Hammond returns to the precinct with an ice pack over his right hand as he sits at his desk. He thought of where Bronson Metger could hide, not to mention Alex's known whereabouts. Captain Railsback stops by to check up on his young Detective.

"You seem tired, Boyce," he says, "are you alright?"

"No, Captain," Hammond replies. "I wish I could crack the Metger case wide open. It's hard to figure where he is, so I can bust him."

"That may work on TV, but it doesn't work in this precinct."

"I know, Captain, but this creep is four steps ahead of us, which makes it harder for us to find him."

"I know, but if Metger finds out Alex is not back in Michigan, he won't stop until she's dead."

"It's also why I want to stop him," Hammond says as he hears the phone ring. "On top of that, I have to answer the phone."

Hammond picks up the phone.

"San Dimas Police, Hammond speaking."

The call comes from Harold S. Palmer, Attorney-at-Law. Hammond is not in a good mood.

"What do you want, you worthless piece of slime!"

"Detective, I want to talk to you about Metger."

"What makes you so sure I don't spill hot coffee on you, again?"

"Because I'm turning myself in."

"WHAT!"

"If you think I'm lying, look outside the precinct."

Hammond leaves his office and sees Palmer standing outside the precinct's door.

Palmer says, "Would a guilty man run, Detective?"

Palmer placed his hands in front of him as Hammond slaps on the cuffs and reads the shyster lawyer his rights.

***

Moments later, Hammond interrogates Palmer.

"Now tell me, why did you turn yourself in after what's been done?"

"Do you remember the time you arrested Maxine," Palmer says, "after she fired me, I contacted Metger to make sure she doesn't work with you in finding him."

"So you called Bronson Metger to kill Maxine at her home," Hammond says. "Forget it! I'm not buying what you're saying."

"Say what you want to say, Mr. Hammond, but I am telling you the truth."

"Hammond isn't pulling any punches on Palmer, even if what the crooked lawyer isn't fabricating what he said.

"I know you're a sick, twisted little worm who should be arrested by the Fashion Police," he says. "There's no way a creep like you can conspire with a psychotic stalker like Bronson Metger."

"Detective Hammond, I don't care if you call me any name in the book," Palmer says. "I am those things, maybe more."

"Why on Earth did you come to my precinct and tell me you surrender?"

"Because I'm afraid for my life, Detective. If Bronson knows I've come to help you, he'll kill me like he killed Maxine."

Hammond still thinks Palmer is lying, but he needs to find a way of revealing it. He has a brilliant idea.

"Would you consider taking a polygraph test?"

Palmer goes into a panic. "What are you, crazy! I'm begging for my life, and you still think I'm lying!"

"If you're telling the truth about Metger planning on killing you, we need to be sure," Hammond says. "If you're lying, I'll throw you to the path of an oncoming bus. Now, are you thinking about taking a lie detector test?"

Palmer had no choice but to take Hammond's request.

"Alright, Detective, you win. I'll take the lie detector test," he says. "But if the test proves I'm telling the truth, I demand you apologize to me."

"No promises, I'll get our administrator to set it up," Hammond replies. "In the meantime, you'll be in a cell until we're ready."

Hammond gets an officer to take the crooked lawyer to his cell. As he contacts the examiner to bring the polygraph, Captain Railsback knows his Detective is worrying.

"I know that look, Boyce," he says, "you still think he's lying?"

Hammond answers, "Can you find me one honest lawyer in all of San Dimas, Captain?"

"I don't think there's any honest lawyer in the greater Los Angeles area," Railsback replies. "They're the ones who get the most money."

"Palmer won't be enjoying it once he's behind bars."

As Hammond walks away, Railsback says to himself the only way he knows.

"For your sake, Boyce. I hope you're right."

***

An hour later, Palmer took the polygraph test. The administrator placed the shyster in the hot seat and hooked him with every wire around his body. He started asking questions about Metger, Maxine, and even Dr. Birney to Palmer. Every time Palmer answers each question, the needles don't move one inch. As the test ends, Palmer returns to his cell. The examiner shows the results to Hammond and Captain Railsback. The two brought Palmer back to the interrogation room. Hammond has only one thing to say to the shyster.

"Congratulations, you passed."

A smile ran across Palmer's face as he heard the news. Hammond continues figuring out more on his test.

"What surprises me is that you didn't use any countermeasures," he says. "How come?"

"I've read reports on how people beat polygraphs by using countermeasures and wise tales," Palmer explains to the Detective. "I wanted to prove I have nothing to hide."

Hammond adds one little detail, "You also know that a polygraph test is not admissible when you're in court."

"I do, and I also know I'll never practice law again after I turn myself in."

"You may get a chance at redemption, Palmer," Railsback says, "if you can tell us one thing."

"Which is?"

Hammond looks at the crooked lawyer with one question in mind.

"When was the last time you talked with Bronson Metger?"

Palmer told everything he knew the last time he talked with Metger. He also tells Hammond when he spies on Alex whether from her job or at home. He also contacts Metger telling him where Alex is.

"All the time you spied on Alex, did you kill Detective Reed Lovell?" Hammond asked.

"No, I may be a shyster, but I'm not a murderer," Palmer says. "I have a big file on Dr. Birney in my office if you insist on seeing it."

"I'll get a search warrant and look for it myself," Hammond replies. "In the meantime, you must stay in your cell for a while."

As he takes Palmer to jail, Hammond gets a search warrant and heads to Palmer's office. When he got there, the office looked like an earthquake destroyed the place. The glass door shattered as if somebody busted in. Hammond contacts the technicians from the crime lab to come to Palmer's office, in the hopes they would find some evidence to capture Bronson Metger.

Chapter 20

Hours passed as lab technicians came in gathering clues from the law office of Harold S. Palmer, Attorney-at-Law. Boyce Hammond stands there wondering why Bronson Metger would trash Palmer's office, where he knows an interior decorator couldn't make the place look good. The lab technician tells Hammond what happened here.

"All in all, I thought an earthquake came in and trashed the place."

"More like an aftershock, Weiss," Hammond says. "If an earthquake came here, this office would be swallowed whole."

Another technician might have found a big clue.

"Detective, do you think somebody would call the place?"

"Feldman, no human being on this planet would ever call this place," Hammond says.

"What about the answering machine?" Feldman replies. "There might be a few messages from it?"

"No offense, Will," Hammond replies, "They wouldn't call this place even for a good time. Take it and see who's been calling Palmer."

Hammond talks to Samantha Bakker, as she checks the broken glass from Palmer's door.

"Anything on the door?"

"I spotted some blood on the glass," she says. "The suspect must have had his arm cut from it."

Hammond replies, "Whoever broke in got cut when trying to reach the doorknob."

As the technicians gather the evidence from Palmer's messy office, a janitor comes in with a cart demanding what's going on.

"What is the meaning of this?" she asks in a furious tone. "Why are you raiding Mr. Palmer's office?"

Detective Hammond flashes his badge to the janitor.

"We like to ask you a few questions, Miss..."

"Helga, Helga Von Alpha," she says. "Now, answer me, what are you doing in Mr. Palmer's office?"

"This is a police matter, ma'am. Somebody ransacked the place."

Helga couldn't believe what happened. She starts cursing up a storm in German. Hammond tries to get a word in.

"Ma'am, I don't understand what you're saying."

"Unless you speak German, you need to wash my mouth with soap," the janitor says. "Could you let me clean Mr. Palmer's office?"

"I'm sorry, but you can't clean here ma'am," Hammond replies. "This is a crime scene, and it'll be off-limits until further notice."

Helga leaves the hallway, cursing in German. Hammond knows Metger got involved breaking into Palmer's office and getting the files on Alex. If he finds out what Palmer has on Dr. Birney, she would be in serious jeopardy. Hammond decides to have one more conversation with Harold S. Palmer, Attorney-at-Law.

***

"Ransacked! How can that be!"

Those words came from the mouth of Harold Palmer as Boyce Hammond told him what happened to his office.

"When I got in, someone busted your door down like a bull in a china shop."

"I couldn't believe Metger would do that," Palmer says, "I told him what I found, and I would give it to him in a few days."

"There's no honor among thieves, Palmer," Hammond says. "I hate to be the one to say it, but when you're dealing with Bronson Metger, he doesn't enjoy waiting."

"Tell me about it. I never thought murder would be his solution."

"He already murdered three people, Palmer," Hammond says. "How many more people will he kill because they stood in his way?"

Palmer sat in silence without having an answer. He thought about what consequences it would bring when Bronson Metger runs all over San Dimas looking for Alex Birney. Hammond has one thing to say to the crooked lawyer.

"For your sake, Mr. Palmer, you better pray to God that Alex Birney is still alive when I take down Bronson Metger."

An officer takes Palmer back to his cell. Hammond stays in the interrogation room alone while Metger is somewhere over San Dimas laughing maniacally.

***

For Boyce Hammond, the case is harder to crack than a walnut with a tough shell. He knows Alex is not in Tecumseh and might be somewhere around the area. He also knows Bronson Metger is still in San Dimas looking for Alex. Captain Railsback comes to Hammond's desk and has an idea which the detective might not like.

"Boyce, you look tired," he says, "why don't you go home and rest for a few days."

"I can't, Captain," Hammond says. "If I'm off the case, Alex will be in great danger."

"I know, but the problem is this case is going nowhere," Railsback replies. "Metger keeps being one step ahead of us, and I'm sick of this as much as you are."

Hammond brings his two cents to the table. "I understand, Captain. The other problem is that every time I try to find Metger, he keeps sending decoys like Waggoner and Palmer to keep me distracted."

Railsback has one more piece of advice to give to his detective.

"Remember, Boyce. It's not how Metger is doing this to you; it's why he's doing it."

"I understand the how, Captain," Hammond replies, "but why would he look for Alex while he would kill others who might turn on him?"

"It's more like setting up the mousetrap, and you notice the cheese is gone while the trap is still set," Railsback says. "You later find out you don't have a mouse, you have a rat."

Hammond thought of what his supervisor said, and an idea popped into his head.

"Mousetrap, that's it!"

"What do you mean, Hammond?"

"You said about setting a mousetrap, and Metger finds a way of getting the cheese without getting caught."

"Of course, but how does it involve Metger?"

"I have one last chance to stop Metger, Captain," Hammond answered, "I need to make this count."

Hammond contacts the tech lab to bring the equipment he found from the Snowball's Chance Motel and orders them to take it to KPDC radio within one hour. Railsback seems confused with what his detective plans on doing.

"Hammond, what on Earth are you doing?"

Hammond replies, "I'm building a better mousetrap. The radio station is where it began, and I'm planning on ending it tonight."

"What makes you sure Metger will fall for it?"

Hammond turns to his supervisor and says, "Because I know what he wants. I want to be the one to trap him."

Railsback responds, "Do whatever it takes, Hammond. I want this case closed!"

"Yes, sir," Hammond says with a smile.

"I'll get you a warrant for Metger's arrest," Railsback says as he leaves Hammond's workstation.

Hammond picks up his phone and calls a number he kept on his wallet. The phone rings on the other line as Hammond waits for the recipient to answer. As he hears a hello from the other end, Hammond gives his response to his caller.

"It's time."

Who was Hammond calling to say it's time? Why did he keep the number in mind? Does he have a plan to stop Bronson Metger? All the questions will be answered when Boyce Hammond goes back to where the crime started. Hoping he might stop Bronson Metger once and for all.

Chapter 21

It's 11:45 PM, fifteen minutes until the witching hour. Boyce Hammond arrives at the parking lot of KPDC radio awaiting his last encounter with Bronson Metger. The tech van had arrived earlier, preparing to help with Hammond's mousetrap.

"We got the stuff from the motel like you said, Boyce," said Lester, "we're ready when you are."

"Have you guys set the equipment up?" Hammond asked.

"Almost ready, sir," Lester replies, "the DJ might want to have a word with you."

Hammond knows what Lester is talking about. A few minutes earlier, Maniac continued his broadcast when he saw the tech lab bringing the equipment for Operation: Mousetrap. Maniac never heard about it; the technician tells him to talk to Detective Hammond about it. Maniac would be happy to ask what Hammond has in mind.

Hammond and Lester enter the front door of the station. A receptionist continues to read the latest Preston Dameron novel without a chance of telling the detective and the lead technician to stop where they're at. Lester couldn't believe what took place.

"You know something, Boyce," he says. "I thought she would stop us."

"For a moment, Les, I thought she did."

Boyce and Lester head to the elevator to the studio. They both saw Maniac Mike Martinez with a concerned look on his face.

"Detective Hammond, you know that Dr. Birney is not here."

"I know, Maniac, which is why I'm here."

"Why are you here in the studio?"

"Because this is where the case started, Mike. And tonight, I am here to end it."

Maniac smiles with what Hammond had in mind, but he asked one more question.

"How are you going to lure Bronson Metger out of hiding?"

Hammond tells the nighttime shock-jock what he has in mind.

"I'm here to build one heck of a mousetrap."

"Impossible," Maniac says, "we don't have any mice in the station."

"No, but you have a dirty stinking rat loose in San Dimas," Hammond replies, "for this, you need to have the right bait."

"How are you going to do that?"

Hammond asks the shock jock his question, "What time is it now?"

Maniac looks at the clock, knowing it's five minutes till midnight.

"Oh, crap!" he shouts, "I have to sign off!"

Maniac goes back to the studio, Hammond follows him.

"Well, my fellow lunatics, it's time for me to go back to the funny farm. So stay tuned for more music until the sun comes up right here on KPDC. Until we meet again, the asylum is on lockdown."

Maniac lets out a laugh once the music plays. The tech lab set up the laptop in the engineering room. Hammond asked the tech boys if everything's ready and gives one last piece of advice.

"Remember, we have one shot at stopping Metger. We need to make this count."

Lester answers, "Will do."

Maniac is still in the dark with what Operation: Mousetrap is and what Hammond has in mind with what the technicians are doing. It's getting close to midnight, and as the seconds continue to tick away, Hammond gives one more piece of advice. This time, the advice is for Maniac.

"Now, Maniac, I want to warn you what I'm gonna do may shock you."

"Detective, you said it yourself," Maniac replies, "I'm a shock jock, nothing would shock me."

"I believe what you're about to see will. Trust me."

The clock strikes midnight, and Detective Boyce Hammond sits in the disc jockey's chair and waits for Maniac to turn on the mike. Maniac listens from the engineer's room as he hears Hammond speak.

"It's midnight, and it's time for you to confess. Welcome to the return of 'Midnight Confessions.' I'm your host, Dr. Alexandria Birney, and tonight is a special edition of 'Midnight Confessions.' It's for an audience of one."

Maniac Mike Martinez couldn't believe what he saw and heard. He saw Boyce Hammond on the microphone, but his ears heard the voice of Dr. Alexandria Birney. He asks a question to the technician.

"Am I hallucinating? I thought I heard Alex's voice."

The technician replies, "You're not hallucinating. We found a program in Metger's laptop that can make him change his voice into anybody he chooses."

"Including the creepy stalker?"

"Exactly," Lester replies, "all we're doing now is fight fire with fire."

Maniac is surprised to see what has taken place, but he thought if Bronson Metger would think of listening to the radio and hear Alex's voice again. Hammond turns on the heat.

"Bronson, I know you're listening, and you want to talk to me. I want you to hear me out. Meet me on the rooftop of the station. I know you can be there to do a simple task. Come on, Bronson. I miss you; we need to make up for lost time."

Hammond gives the nod to the engineer to play music as Maniac wants to know how Hammond pulled off a potential practical joke on Metger.

"I can't believe what you did, Detective," he says, "you're talking like Alex to get Metger. It's impossible!"

"I got one shot to bring Metger down, Maniac," Hammond says with a smile. "I hope tonight will be the night we put them behind bars, for good."

"What do you want me to do?"

"Entertain them," Hammond says as he leaves the studio.

"Entertain them?" Maniac says in confusion. "How can I entertain them by being a woman?"

***

Outside the station, a car with a Michigan license plate arrives at the parking lot. Bronson Metger steps out of the car with a gun behind his back. He's unaware that a trap is being sent for him. He goes inside en route to the roof of the station. As Metger enters the station, another car approaches in the parking lot. The driver parked the car alongside Metger's and turned off the engine. The stranger sits in the car and looks at a text that reads this message.

"Wait until I give you the signal, then come to the roof."

The stranger sits in the car in the hopes of what's coming. The stranger sends a text saying:

"I am here and waiting for the word."

The stranger waits for another text from the mysterious benefactor to give the signal. About two minutes of waiting, the stranger receives a message on the phone saying it's time. The stranger gets out of the car and heads to the studio. Unaware that the receptionist is still reading her book. Phase one is over; how to get to the roof is another story. The stranger thought the elevators were under protection by the station's security. The stranger takes the stairs leading to the roof.

***

Within minutes, Bronson Metger arrives at the roof of KPDC radio. The height of the building, not to mention the dark, late-night sky, is giving the obsessed stalker a slight sense of vertigo. Where are you, Alex? He thought as he couldn't stand being alone on the roof in the middle of the night.

"I'm here, Alex; where are you!"

Hammond awaits in the shadows, calling the number on Metger's cell phone. As Metger's phone rings, he quickly answers the phone.

"Alex, is it you, baby?"

"It's me, Bronson. I knew you would come."

Metger doesn't know he's the victim of Hammond's revenge as the detective is using Metger's voice changing software on his cell phone. He believes that using a sample of Alex's voice would attract Metger like flies to honey.

"Baby, where are you?" Metger asked, "I'm worried sick about you."

Hammond continues the charade.

"Oh, I know, sweetie," he says, "but I can't come back to Michigan."

"Why not! I love you; you don't know what I did for you."

"You mean like busting out of prison, killing somebody, and stealing a car to come and find me."

"But Alex, it was all out of love."

"Love? You don't know what love is, Bronson."

Metger keeps looking around for Alex. He's not aware of Hammond hiding in the shadows.

"C'mon, Alex, don't play games with me."

"Moi, I thought you enjoyed being on top of the world."

"Not when it's late at night, and I'm terrified of heights."

"You said you're the king, baby. I still think you're a coward."

Metger gets furious as Hammond laughs in Alex's voice.

"I ain't no coward, you ungrateful tramp!" Metger shouted, "I have the right to kill you if you don't show yourself right now!"

Hammond thinks the time has come to spring the trap on Bronson Metger.

"Of course, you have the right, baby..."

Hammond turns off the voice changer on his phone and says what Metger doesn't want to hear.

"You have the right to remain silent."

Metger couldn't believe his ears. He laughs at what he heard on the phone.

"Oh, Alex. I don't think you would tell me I have the right to remain silent."

Hammond is serious about what he said.

"If you give up the right to remain silent," he continued, "anything you say can and will be used against you in a court of law."

Metger gets angry.

"Where are you, you witch! Show yourself to me right now!"

"You have the right to an attorney and have an attorney present while questioning."

Metger comes to his senses when he finds out he's not talking to Dr. Birney on the phone.

"Wait, a minute; you're not Alex," he says. "You're the cop from the motel, the one who stole my stuff."

Hammond points his gun behind Metger.

"Your stuff is evidence in a crime, Metger," he says, "and if you cannot afford an attorney, one will be provided for you. Do you now understand your rights?"

Metger turns around and gives a sarcastic response to the young detective.

"You forgot the only right I still have," he says, "I have the right to kick your..."

Metger sucker-punches Hammond in the gut, which causes him to drop his gun. Metger also gives his rival a roundhouse kick to the head. As Hammond tries to get his gun off the ground, Metger kicks it to the side, making sure it's out of reach. He quickly takes his gun out from behind his back and points it at Hammond. Hammond slowly tries to get up, but Metger has other plans for the detective.

"Uh-uh-uh, copper," he says. "You better stay down if you care about living."

Metger pulls the hammer of his gun, cocking it back while pointing the barrel at Hammond as he tries to get up. Hammond had one chance to stop Alex's crazed stalker, but without his sidearm, he's a sitting duck. Metger gets ready to pull the trigger on Boyce Hammond. Before Bronson Metger could ever get a shot, somebody shot the gun out of Metger's hand like a scene from the westerns. Metger curses like crazy as he held his hand in pain. Hammond looks at who shot the gun off Metger's hand. He realizes who it was by the baseball cap she's wearing and knew she's walking into a different trap.

"Alex," he says, "you shouldn't have come back."

It was Alex Birney, holding Hammond's gun with her sights set on killing Bronson Metger.

"I'm sorry, Boyce," she replies, "but this crap ends tonight."

Metger couldn't believe seeing Alex.

"Alex," he says, "you've come back to me at last."

As he tries to hug his old girlfriend, Alex points the gun on Metger, forcing him to back off.

"Don't you dare take one step, Bronson," she says in anger. "I swear to God if you do, you'll be dead!"

Hammond gets up and attempts to play peacemaker.

"Alex, give me the gun," he says. "I don't want you to be vengeful."

"I'm sorry, Boyce," Alex replies, "but tonight is where it ends."

"I can't let you take Metger's life this way, Alex," Hammond says. "He needs to go back and face trial in Michigan."

"I ain't going back to Michigan," Metger says, "I want to stay with my true love."

Alex protests, "Forget it, Bronson. The only way you're going back to Michigan is in a coffin."

As Metger takes another step forward, Alex shoots. Hammond takes Alex's arm, so she shoots up instead.

"Boyce!" she shouted, "What are you doing!"

"I can't allow you to kill Metger," Hammond says. "He needs to stand trial in Michigan."

"So he can get out on a technicality, fat chance!"

"Alex, I know he hurts you. I don't believe it's right for you to take the law into your own hands."

Alex disagrees, "It's more than an obsession, Boyce. I don't want the nightmare to continue."

"It will never continue, Alex; I'll make sure of it," Hammond says. "Please, Alex. Give me the gun."

Alex gives Hammond the gun. Hammond gives her respect.

"You did the right thing, Alex."

Alex sheds a tear and hugs her protector. As Hammond tries to embrace her, Metger strikes back like a venomous rattlesnake as he wraps Alex with one arm and holds a switchblade knife in the other. Hammond points the gun at Metger, but Metger threatens the detective.

"Stand down, Detective! Stand down, or I'll kill her!"

"Let her go, Metger!" Hammond shouted. "You've already done enough damage!"

"You fool! You're the reason Alex doesn't love me!"

"You're wrong, Bronson! You want to control her like a puppet. Anything to satisfy your needs."

"Shut up! I don't want to hear about it!"

"Look around you, Metger! We're on the roof of a radio station; you try to head off with Alex, and they'll be cops on the ground floor waiting for your arrest."

"It's never going to happen," Metger says, "I'll leave with what I wanted since high school. My future wife."

"I'll never marry you if you were the last psycho on Earth," Alex says. "You need to let me go!"

"Be quiet when I'm talking, you tramp!" Metger says. "It's your fault for keeping me away from you."

"You're obsessive, Metger," Hammond replies. "You want Alex to be your property."

"I said shut up, you flatfoot!"

"She's a human being for crying out loud!" Hammond shouted. "Drop the knife and let her go, right now!"

Metger continues to hold Alex as his hostage, trying to get out of the radio station's rooftop when he sees a helicopter circling the station like a vulture circling a dead carcass. The helicopter shines a bright light that blinds him. A voice from the loudspeakers blare out a warning.

"Attention Bronson Metger, this is the San Dimas Police Department. We have the building surrounded. Release your hostage and place your hands above your head. You are under arrest."

Metger shouted, "You did this! You called the police!"

Hammond replies, "I did nothing. I'm surprised they would show up."

Metger then turns to Alex, "It was you, you ungrateful tramp!"

Alex says, "How would I call the police when you have me as a hostage."

Hammond looked down and saw the mother of all standoffs. Squad cars from the San Dimas Police Department, the Los Angeles County Sheriff's Department, and the California Highway Patrol surround the station, leaving a flashing sea of red and blue lights.

"Look around you, Metger!" Hammond shouted. "They have the building surrounded."

"SO!"

"So, if you go down with Alex, they'll be ready with two options," Hammond replies. "The first option is they'll be ready with handcuffs."

"What's the second option, Flatfoot?"

Hammond answers, "The second option is they'll kill you, and they'll also kill Alex."

"You're bluffing!" Metger says, "No copper is going to keep me away from my girl."

"You don't get it, Metger," Hammond says. "All she did was to make a personal success for herself. Instead of being jealous and controlling her like a dog, you should be happy and encourage her."

"Shut up!"

"No, you shut up when a real man is talking!" Hammond says, "If you don't believe that you're surrounded, look down. Tell me if I'm lying!"

Metger heads towards the edge while holding on to Alex and sees a group of squad cars like Hammond told him before.

"You think your police buddies are gonna stop me," he says. "You're going to tell them to stand down and let us pass through. I'm going to take her to Vegas."

"Forget it, Bronson," Alex says as she struggles to break free. "I'm not going anywhere with you."

"That's no way to talk to your soon-to-be husband, Alex."

Out of nowhere, Metger's cell phone rings. Hammond has to get Metger to answer it.

"Aren't you gonna pick up the phone?" he asked. "All you have to do is release your victim."

Metger believes it is another trap set up by Hammond.

"You pick it up," he replies, "I have my hands full."

"There's no need for you to be rude," Hammond replies, "I'll be happy to pick it up."

Hammond heads to Metger's phone while pointing his gun at the criminal. He picks the phone up from the ground and answers.

"Hello."

The person on the other line wants to talk to Metger. Hammond couldn't believe his ears, but played along.

"Yes, Metger is here."

The mysterious caller wants Hammond to put Metger on the phone.

"Bronson," he says, "someone wishes to speak with you."

"Who, my mother?" Metger replies. "She never understood me."

"This is serious, Metger," Hammond says, "somebody wants to talk to you right now."

Metger couldn't believe what Hammond said. He gives in and tells Hammond what to do.

"Put it on speakerphone."

Hammond tells the caller one last detail.

"I'm going to place this call on speakerphone," he says. "The next voice you'll hear will be Bronson Metger's."

Hammond turns on the speaker and hands the phone over to Metger. He retracts the knife out of his hand and places it in his front pocket while he continues to hold Alex with his arm around her neck.

"Hello," he answers.

"Bronson, why did you do what you did?"

In a surprising moment, Bronson Metger goes from being maniacal to being frozen stiff. Because from that moment in time, he heard the voice of Maxine Hathaway on the other line.

"No, this can't be possible, you're dead!"

"What's wrong, Metger?" Hammond asks. "You look like you've heard the voice of a ghost."

"Why did you kill me, Bronson," the ghostly caller says. "Why did you threaten me?"

"Shut up! Shut up! Shut up!" Metger says in an angry tone. "I killed you! You're dead!"

"Wrong, Metger," the caller replies. "It's you who will die for all the sins you committed."

"I don't want to hear it! I killed you! You're DEAD!"

Metger drops the phone as he goes into a fit of rage as he holds on to Alex. Hammond tells him one last ultimatum.

"That's enough, Metger. Let Alex go or I will shoot!"

"If I die, Alex will join me for all eternity."

Alex replies, "No... I... WON'T!"

Alex breaks free from her deadly stalker. First, she stomps on his foot with tremendous force. Metger screams at the pain. Then Alex elbows Metger right in the gut, causing him to loosen his grip. Finally, Alex frees herself by taking her fist and hitting her ex-boyfriend in the family jewels. Once Alex escaped from Metger's clutches, Hammond shot three bullets to Metger's chest. The force from the bullets made Metger stumble to the ledge and fall to his doom. Hammond gazed over to see the splattered remains of Bronson Metger. Alex wants to look, but Hammond told her not to. As the young detective holds Alex, they both hear a voice coming from the speaker of Metger's cell phone.

"How did I do, Alex?"

It was Maniac, pretending to be Maxine on the phone to trick Metger. Alex picks up the phone and tells the shock jock what she thinks of his performance.

"Maniac, you were awesome!"

Hammond couldn't believe what Maniac Mike Martinez pulled off to play the hero.

"Maniac, you have a lot of explaining to do."

"It's best I explain to both of you downstairs," Maniac replies. "I don't think your boss would believe what happened, Detective."

"We'll see you then, Maniac. Bye."

As Hammond hangs up the phone, he looks at Alex and says, "Care to go inside?"

Alex replies, "I thought you never asked."

Alex kisses her brave hero right on the lips. Hammond becomes flustered.

"I'm surprised I didn't frisk you."

The two giggled as they head downstairs, getting ready to explain their story to Maniac and a concerned Captain Railsback.

***

As Hammond and Alex head downstairs, they see Maniac and Captain Railsback waiting for them. They both have different reactions.

"I like to know why you had to bring Alex back here, Hammond," Railsback says. "I thought she was back in Michigan."

"We wanted Metger to think Alex went back to Michigan to find him quick," Hammond replies. "Alex never went to Michigan to begin with."

"What do you mean, never?"

Alex gives Railsback her explanation.

"When we got to the airport, I had my ticket ready for my flight to Detroit," she says. "I saw a guy who wanted to see his wife in Detroit. He found out she went into labor."

"Did he get to go?" Asked the Captain.

"The flight from Los Angeles to Detroit was full," Alex replies, "I gave him my ticket."

"What you did, Dr. Birney was generous of you," Railsback says, "but where were you when we search for your obsessed ex-boyfriend?"

"I spent the next few days at a homeless shelter which a friend of Boyce ran," Alex replies, "I love helping some who are not as fortunate. Boyce keeps texting me from time to time, asking if I'm alright."

"I even text her saying it's time when we were going to catch Metger," Hammond says. "The question I like to know is who called you guys to surround the station?"

Railsback answered, "You can thank Maniac for that, Hammond."

Maniac replies, "The truth is, I have to give credit to Alex. When she arrived at the studio, she told me to contact the police."

"What about Maxine's voice?" Hammond asks, "I thought I heard a ghost when you called Metger's phone."

Maniac gives his explanation, "When you did the beginning of 'Midnight Confessions' mimicking Alex's voice on the air, I thought Alex is back for real."

"Even I took the shock as well too," Railsback says. "From that time, Alex is pretty sneaky. I didn't expect you to be like Alex, Hammond."

Maniac continues, "So, I asked your friend from the tech lab to install the mimic app on my new cell phone."

Hammond couldn't believe what he heard from Maniac.

"When did you get a new cell phone, Maniac?"

"I got it over the weekend," Maniac replies, "I don't use it often, but when they installed the program Metger used, I didn't want anybody to mess with Alex or anybody else in the station. Now I have to go back to the tech boys to uninstall it."

"Sorry, Maniac," Hammond replies, "I don't want you to use it the same way Metger did."

Railsback instructs his top detective, "I want a full report on my desk tomorrow."

"I'll do that, Captain."

"In the meantime, I want you to take Alex home," Railsback says. "Now the case is over; it'll be best for Dr. Birney to lie down in her bed."

Alex threw her own two cents, "After what I've been through, I also need a hot shower."

"I believe I can take you home, Alex," Hammond replies.

"Go exit through the back," Railsback says, "the press has the front exit blocked."

Hammond and Alex left the radio station using the rear exit and got into Hammond's car. They got out of the parking lot before any of the reporters try to get an exclusive interview.

***

Moments later, Hammond took Alex back to her apartment. She can now breathe a sigh of relief, knowing that Bronson Metger is no longer a threat in her young life.

"Boyce, I wanted to say thank you," she says. "I wouldn't know what you'd do if Bronson killed me."

"Don't worry about it, Alex," Hammond replies, "the best thing you can do now is take a good hot shower and get some sleep."

"I'm going to be so happy sleeping in my bed for a change," said Alex as she opens the door. "Would you like to stay for a nightcap?"

"I love to, but I have to file my report to Captain Railsback first thing."

"I guess a detective's work is never done."

"No, but I'm free tomorrow night."

Alex smiles at the news. She gives Hammond a kiss which is slow but passionate.

"Until tomorrow, thank you. Thank you for everything."

"No, thank you for knowing I'm not too stubborn," Hammond says as he kisses Alex. "Goodnight, Alex."

"Goodnight, Boyce."

As Hammond heads back to his car to go home, Alex enters her apartment. She turns on the lights as she sits down on the couch and cries. Alex grabs the nearest pillow she could find as she turns on the waterworks. She cried for the reason she's happy to be alive after what she's been through. Happy because Alex Birney can now live on with her own life.

Epilogue

A few months passed after the Metger affair. Alex Birney became a local celebrity. Her practice is getting major clientele throughout the county. Her show, 'Midnight Confessions' is airing all over the greater Los Angeles area with talks of having the show syndicated nationwide within the year.

Boyce Hammond finished his report on the Metger case, and within a couple of weeks, he rose to the rank of Sergeant. The youngest in the history of the San Dimas Police Department. He also became the lead investigator in several cases throughout San Dimas and the greater Los Angeles area.

After the Metger case, Harold S. Palmer lost his license to practice law. He is now running security in a strip mall outside the city limits.

James Waggoner is on probation and got a job afterward. He works alongside Zeus as a bouncer at the Wrecking Ball.

Maniac Mike Martinez is still causing his own brand of trouble. The trouble he causes is when he's on the air. Off the air, he's normal, unless he's dealing with a bunch of rowdy fans whenever they see him. He continues to be Alex's lead-in on KPDC radio, where he continues to be rambunctious and makes a shocking announcement.

"Well, folks, I would tell you to stick around for Dr. Alex Birney and her hot show 'Midnight Confessions,'" he says, "instead you're going to stick with me until the crack of dawn. Because over the weekend, our own Dr. Birney got married to Sergeant Boyce Hammond of the San Dimas Police Department."

***

Halfway around the world, the newlyweds are on their honeymoon listening to Maniac's broadcast on Alex's smartphone app. Maniac continues to tell more stories from their wedding.

"Unfortunately for me, I was the one who caught the bouquet. I'm still embarrassed about it. Anyway, congratulations to the two of you."

Alex lies in her lounge chair in a sky blue bikini, gazing over the bright blue sky over Bora Bora as Hammond comes back from the bar with a couple of mimosas.

"Here you go, honey," he says as he kissed his new bride.

"Here's to us," Alex says as the two give cheers.

"So, Mrs. Hammond, how does it feel to be married?"

"I was going to ask you the same question, Mr. Birney."

Hammond laughs at his new wife's remarks, but later kisses and make-up.

"So, Boyce, what do you want to do tonight?"

"I thought of chartering a boat and doing some skin diving to see the turtles," Boyce replies.

Alex has an idea of her own.

"How about after that, we go back to our bungalow for some room service, and I'll give you the sexiest massage you'll ever have."

"Baby," Hammond answers, "I'll drink to that."

The newlyweds clink their glasses and lock their lips together for a kiss as they watch the gentle breeze swaying the trees and the roaring surf pounding onto the sandy beach, enjoying their unforgettable Tahitian honeymoon. They can now breathe a sigh of relief for the nightmare between them, and Bronson Metger is over, and they now face a new start as husband and wife. Boyce Hammond now knows that finding somebody to love is not found on a mugshot. As for Dr. Alexandria Birney, they were finding her calling means facing your fear and conquering it, whether it's work, or in love. All it takes is a simple confession.